HOOK: WHIRLPOOL OF STARS

Hook: Whirlpool of Stars

TULLY ZETFORD

NEW ENGLISH LIBRARY
TIMES MIRROR

An NEL Original

© Tully Zetford, 1974

*

FIRST NEL PAPERBACK EDITION MAY 1974

*

NEL Books are published by The New English Library Limited from Barnard's Inn, Holborn, London E.C.1. Made and printed in Great Britain by C. Nicholls & Company Ltd.

45001838 5

CHAPTER ONE

HOOK had never been more aware of the intolerance of the galaxy whirling and glittering away outside than in this very instant as the starship's engines ripped themselves to shreds. A fracture the size of a micro-dot split the shielding. From that molecule-wide gap a beam of lethally-hard radiation spurted lengthwise through the ship. It lasted for a tenth of a second. In that time it destroyed the ship utterly.

A big beefy man smoking a cigar spoke to Hook as the engines blew. The next instant as the radiation beam sliced zig-zag through the man, he collapsed to the decking. His body had been cut into a dozen separate pieces.

Hook stepped aside, cursing the engine-room crew. They were a bunch of good-for-nothing slobs. The catastrophic failure of the engines proved the crew inefficient; and inefficiency in any form upset Ryder Hook. This time some regurgitated womb-fugitive's slackness was like to get Ryder Hook killed.

The annunciator system said: "All passengers to C Deck. All passen –" And stopped. It never enunciated again.

The ship's artificial gravity which normally kept a comfortable eighth of a g throughout the vessel went mad. Hook's feet left the floor and he floated clear in free-fall. With a slamming shock that jarred his teeth he smashed back to the deck. He judged the artificial gravity to have climbed to six gees. People were falling and screaming everywhere. They were pasted to the deck. Hook started to run for the exit onto C Deck and the life shell racked there.

The gravity peaked and surged and passengers ran and collapsed. No single man could ever help them all out before the ship opened onto space. Sections of the deckhead crumpled as the gravities piled on. A jagged edge broke free and bonged against the deck. Hook vaulted it and a second huge chunk split with screech and hammered down on him.

5

He skidded flat on his back, the metal ironing him out, felt the bulkhead come up and sledge him across the back of the head. He lay there for a moment, cursing all the stupid no-good fumble-fingered drive engineers in Creation. If he didn't reach the life shells within minutes he needn't bother about anything else any more.

A little woman from Cailiang, her facial fur dyed orange and indigo, her slit-eyes green with fear, screamed. Her legs were trapped beneath the adjoining sheet. Hook leaned across and said: "Hold your breath, sweetheart," and pulled. He dragged her out, ignoring her shrieks. The last six centimetres of her tail snapped off, snagged by the jagged metal edge.

"Better a chunk of your tail than all of you," said Ryder Hook, and gave her a savage push towards the exit onto C Deck. He put both hands onto the metal edge pinning his thighs.

At that instant the artificial gravity kicked in a last dying surge and the needle shot right off the scale. Hook judged with that steady undeviating portion of his brain that gravity had peaked past twelve gees. A thick construction member in the overhead broke free under that intolerable force. The solid bar of metal drove downwards.

It struck across both his legs with force enough to have smashed clear through armour-steel.

It bounced.

Ryder Hook grunted and heaved the sheet away. The artifical gravity died with that last fenzied surge and the sheet sailed off down the corridor. Hook got his feet under him. He could feel the pain of that solid beam of metal slogging into his legs; but he ignored it. He sprang in a long low dive that took him like a bird towards the exit.

He hoicked the little furred woman from Cailiang with him as he went.

He'd never visited her planet in this wide galaxy; but he'd heard they brewed a sweet-mist there that curled your toes with pleasure. The ship lurched. Most of the primary and secondary lighting circuits had blown and the tertiary emergencies came on with a sickly yellow-green radiance that, in an image as old as Old Earth herself and still as true, turned all their faces corpse-grey.

6

Pandemonium raged up on C Deck. Above the yells and shrieks the senseless siren-wail of the alarm signal continued to belabour ears. That, Hook knew only too well, merely re-inforced panic. Into the ship's air the penetrating stink of burn-ing insulation filtered like old boots burning on a woodfire. Many passengers had reached the life shells and already banks two and three had jetted free of the ship's flank.

She was – or had been – H.G.L. Starship *Iquique*, for ancient names were remembered on Old Earth as elsewhere in the galaxy. Now she was done for. Before she finally broke up and drifted in an idle spray of wreckage those who struggled for life must leave her. Only the dead would remain.

Four more shells departed. Men and women recoiled from the closing panels of alloy-steel that sealed off the launching bays of two more shells. Hook cast a swift and practised look along the ceiling-mounted tell-tales. There were precious few shells left. Air sighed past his cheeks.

He swung about as the airlock valves clamped immediately to his rear. They sealed off the life shell banks from the rest of the ship. Now no one else would be joining the passengers here. Two more shells jetted.

He picked a shell whose light remained green, indicating it was not filled to capacity yet, and took off.

The furry woman ran shrieking after him, bouncing and gy-rating in free-fall as her pumping legs tossed her high against the overhead. Hook had no reason to care for her welfare. She was a complete stranger. But he had pulled her from under the metal pinning her to the deck, and he had carried her here. With a precise calculation he knew that there was time. He owed her, for saving her life already. Ryder Hook had had to leave tasks unfinished in his life; he had never done so voluntarily and he resented not being able to complete a task to which he had set his hand.

The five seconds it took to jump towards her, grab her, quieten her down and tuck her under his arm, consumed all his reserves of time. He thrust with his booted feet and shot straight for the life shell's door. He was the last. A group of people – human be-ings, humanoids, extra-terrestrials, aliens – mixed up in a panic-stricken bunch managed to squirt themselves into the shell. One

7

large and powerfully-muscled Krifman bellowed and charged for the door, head down. Hook knew the Krifmans of old. They were a race who prided themselves on their toughness, their Spartan attitudes to life, their integrity in the galaxy. A good Krifman was a good friend; a bad Krifman was bad news anywhere. This Krifman wore plate-fabric clothes cut tightly to his body, red and green, and his cap's visor was down. That meant trouble.

The girl he pushed aside yelled and tried to claw her way back to the life shell doorway. Hook gave her a single glance, took in the short dark hair, the ripped glitter-dress, the slim naked legs, and then focussed on the Krifman.

"Get out of my way, you Earth trollop!" shouted the Krifman. He punched the girl in the stomach and she doubled up and fell away, retching. The big man ducked his head to enter the door.

Hook's feet hit the deck. A new alarm screamed into the metal compartment. Air pressure had sunk to danger level; the ship was evacuating and soon her hulk would be one with space.

Hook took the Krifman's shoulder in his right hand and pulled.

He had the leverage with his feet on the floor; the other was in free-fall. The Krifman span back. Hook hurled the Cailiang woman headfirst into the shell. Her lopped tail flip-flopped as she somersaulted, her baggy pantaloons billowing.

It was difficult to breathe.

The Krifman hit the deck and, instantly, was on his feet and charging for Hook.

"Earth curd! Out of my way!"

"You," said Hook to the Earth girl. "Inside. Hurry."

She started to say something. Hook reached out, grabbed her short hair, jerked.

With a scream the girl flew past him into the shell.

As he straightened up Hook extended his boot. The toe caught the Krifman where in an Earthman it would do the most damage. Krifmans were built like that, too.

Hook backed to the life shell door.

The Krifman's yells thinned and attenuated. His face showed an anger and a spite that fear as yet could not touch. He flexed his hand. Hook waited for no more. He caught a single glimpse of the little handgun flicking from the Krifman's sleeve. The life shell door slid to with a comfortingly loud thump. Watching it, Hook saw an apple-sized dome abruptly appear on the inside of the metal. An instant later and that blast would have pushed his backbone out past his ribcage.

With a jolting discharge that rocked everyone inside, the life shell blasted free of *Iquique.*

Hook looked down past the rows of functional seating towards the control section. He caught a glimpse past the screen of an officer's cap. At least the shell was in hands capable of piloting it.

The Earth girl was trying to pull up her ripped shoulder-strap. Her eyes, wide and blue, stared at Hook, and her fingers ceased their fumbling. Her face showed streaked lines of cosmetic powder; but for all that her skin was far whiter than most people's, whose golden tans revealed the many-tangled lines of heritage.

"Thank you," she said. Her voice strengthened as she spoke. "That brute – I'm sorry he died; but –"

Hook jerked a thumb at the tally entry at the port.

Every red dot was alight.

"We're loaded. He was one extra."

"Oh."

They sat side by side in the last pair of seats. The furry female crouched in the next seat, sobbing, exhausted. A woman two seats along was complaining in a loud and hectoring tone.

"All my things! My luggage, my furs, my jewels – all gone!"

Hook saw that she wore a quintuple-string of fire-pearls around her neck, below her three chins. Those three chins came from over-eating, they were not alien, for she was of human parentage. Her highly-coloured face and elaborate coiffure told of her wealth. "My collection of butterfly-jade – all gone! It's disgraceful! I'll complain to H.G.L. the moment we dock!"

The girl at Hook's side laughed.

Of the hundred and twenty five people in the life shell's cabin, Hook surmised, no one had less right to laugh than did he. He felt his thin lips strain. He'd been on the go and on the run without a let-up recently. There were no Boosted Men aboard the shell. He could have done with a Boosted Man nearby during those last hectic moments aboard *Iquique* – then he chilled. Hell! If a Boosted Man knew that Ryder Hook was aboard – exit Ryder Hook.

The girl's laughter faded and she fumbled again with the broken strap of her glitter-dress. Her blue eyes regarded Hook with a look of calculation. The life shell hummed with power circuitry and electronics and the air systems. The conversations of the passengers rose and fell, counter-pointing the noises of the shell.

"What happens next, then, taynor?" Her full lips trembled in the yellow lighting.

"We find a planet and we home in, tayniss," said Hook.

She was clearly of Terrestrial stock, even though she might have been born in any of a hundred thousand solar systems, and Hook fancied that, without disguise, he, too, was clearly of Earthly stock. Yet she had not used mister. She had addressed him with the usual honorific employed out of politeness when talking to any intelligent creature in this segment of the galaxy, and he had replied in kind.

"You've been – that is –" she gestured around the life shell interior. "I just hope we make planetfall safely."

"We'll do that all right," said Hook easily enough. He did not add that their problems would then begin anew.

He'd been spacewrecked before. They might come down on a planet that tolerated human life only a single division above the minimum in the bio-scale. They might face jungles, deserts, ice-caps, hostile aliens, terrors almost inconceivable to the human brain. The equipment coupled onto the shell's computer would sniff out a planet suitable to support human life; it would give no indication of social and environmental conditions upon that planet.

"I'm Pera Sotherton," she said. She shivered. "We will come out of this all right, taynor?"

"The galaxy is a big place," said Hook, and because of that he added: "I'm Ryder Hook. I expect we'll make a good planetfall."

He'd not previously encountered her among the passengers travelling aboard H.G.L. Starship *Iquique*. That was not surprising viewed in terms of the numbers carried, three thousand

10

or so this passage; it was remarkable given her beauty and Hook's eye for a pretty girl.

"I was going to Albeira," she said. Hook saw she wanted to talk. "My boss was called there in a frightful hurry and I'm following him – I was following him."

Hook seldom ever ventured information about himself. Name: – Ryder Hook. Profession: – you name it, he could probably do it himself or find the contact to have it done. Friends: – None – none – none – except, possibly, Shaeel. Shaeel came from Pertan Major, one of the Hermaphrodite planets, and it was just as well ve hadn't been aboard *Iquique* when she blew. Shaeel, like Hook, was a Galactic loner. Home: – where he laid his head. Family: – ah, yes, that was a poser! Aliases: many and varied of which probably the most notorious was Jack Kinch, Galactic Assassin extraordinary. Purpose: – First and foremost to stay alive and keep out of the hands of the Boosted Men, after that, to achieve what he could out of life in this man's galaxy.

An insignificant, a petty, a contemptible set of specifications for a man of the hundred and first century – Old Earth Dating – and yet a set that had kept him alive and operating for as long as this. As the shell picked up a bio-acceptable planet and aligned its limited-life Togossen engines, Hook reflected that he might have been a happier man if he'd simply allowed life to wash over him and bring death as a solution to all his troubles. But Ryder Hook wasn't built in that way. Just so long as a tremor of life flickered in him then just so long would he go on fighting the blind insanity of death and forgetfulness. The whole damned galaxy would have to give in first before he would surrender.

"I was on my way to Coldharbour," he said. The information was now meaningless. "They were keeping a position as electronics consultant open for me."

"I am sorry, Taynor Hook. I hope they don't fill the position before we are rescued." She pronounced taynor with a fullness that showed she had not in her mind used the familiar abridged form of tr. Hook felt she merited tayniss, rather than ts.

The shell buffetted them with gravitic surges from the Togossen engines and Hook heard the off-phase thump of number three. His intolerant hatred of sloppiness and inefficiency must have flared on his face, for Pera Sotherton flinched back.

"What —?"

"The engines," said Hook. "Those tangle-pants of H.G.L. engineers need a bit of smartness knocked into them."

"You'd do the knocking?"

"No need to. I'm a peaceful man, Tayniss Sotherton. I'd just speak to 'em."

"Sooner them than me."

Looking at this stranger by her side, Pera Sotherton knew that she spoke a sober truth. She would give a very great deal not to be in this man's way when he started in on telling somebody a home truth or two. She appraised him, her blue eyes wide.

For all that they were so formally addressing each other as tr. and ts. he was an Earthman as she was an Earthwoman, and for an Earthman he was not overtall, being around two metres in height. He was broad across the shoulders, though, and thick through the chest, and slim around the middle. Pera was not young and silly enough to begin imagining herself being crushed by those thick arms against that massive chest; but the idea undeniably held attractions. This man's eyes and hair were brown. His face bore unmistakably the marks of a rough and tough life, the lips thin, the nose beaked, the chin arrogant. He would be a bad enemy. She wondered if he had found anyone he called friend, and felt that that person, whoever they might be, would be unduly fortunate. Like any other female predator, she had summed him up as a fascinating acquaintance but a dangerous friend and, in all probability, a disastrous partner.

No, decided Miss Pera Sotherton, she would handle this one with radio-active caution.

Mind you, if interesting possibilities came her way, she would dally with them out of a sense of duty to sample the pleasures of the galaxy . . . As a woman that was her right.

She had travelled a long way from Earth. Albeira and her boss lay in the deeps of space ahead, some hundred and eighty or so light years from Earth and *Iquique* had blown short of her destination. Coldharbour, to which this strange man Ryder Hook had been bound, lay closer but still many parsecs away. Just

12

where the life shell would deposit them worried Pera less than what her boss would say, what Hook would do when they arrived – she became aware of a dampness along her forehead and an itch, and she suddenly knew she was very very cross indeed with herself.

With its Togossen engines labouring at full drive the life shell fled across space, swinging in out of the lonely dark and entering a solar system – not the nearest solar system to the wreck but the nearest system containing a planet suitable for human and humanoid life. *Iquique* had been a one-environment ship. She had had no particular compartments set aside for intelligent beings from species who demanded a different set of habitable specifications from the human.

Like a minute speck of iron ore the shell pirouetted around the lines of electro-magnetism pulsing through the system and drove down on the central magnet.

Automatic systems inserted the shell into a stable orbit around the chosen planet.

With a declining thump and a shiver of vibrating metal, the Togossens simmered into silence. People were talking and half-rising from their seats. Hook sat.

He was a man accustomed to forcing himself to sit quietly.

He had often watched caged wild animals – tigers, wildcats, rafils, strackani, eagles – and had perfectly understood their sufferings and the savage impulses burning in them. A man who travelled in space however wild and barbaric his emotions might be must drill and discipline himself to the confining cocoon of alloy-steel and air and electronics. So Ryder Hook just sat inconspicuously and waited for the routine of the docking procedures to release him from the shell.

A customs tender jetted from the surface. She matched orbits and velocities and rode in on the beam. The gentle bump of contact told of her handling capabilities. The airlock cycled and the valves swished open. Men stepped through.

The ship's officer in charge of this life shell walked aft down the gangway to meet the newcomers. He was an anonymous officer who was probably discharging now the most exciting function he would ever be called upon in his career as a starship deck-officer. He checked and a frown appeared on his face. He

13

was young, untested, nervous, with a quiff of blond hair escaping from under his uniform cap. But he knew the drill.

"We're from H.G.L. Starship *Iquique*," he said, in a voice that for all its quaver was courageously firm. "We request all the usual help and assistance afforded spacewreck –"

"Save it, gonil."

The man heading up the customs officers was clad in a one-piece golden coverall. Badges of rank flamed on collar and cuff. He let his right hand rest negligently on the butt of a holstered weapon. It was a Tonota Eighty. Ryder Hook would never miss a detail like that.

"You have chosen to orbit Lerdun. We are a free world."

Cries of pleasure broke from a number of the passengers, who all craned the better to see the outcome of this confrontation. Hook suppressed instantly his feelings of anger and hatred.

"H.G.L. is represented on Lerdun. The Customs man spoke in a short, chopped way, that indicated his own opinion of himself. "All employees and members of H.G.L. will be immediately transported to the surface and will receive every consideration afforded by their credit status."

The fire-pearl-hung woman with the three chins shouted: "And what about the others? I'm Trans-Gal –"

"Trans-Gal? Never heard of them."

"Oh!"

A bristle-haired Riffian, old and ugly, surged up from his seat, his crimson shoulder-cloak flaring, the tranceiver mounted on the bridge of his nose flickering. "I demand –"

"You demand nothing, gonil!" The Customs man gestured. "All H.G.L. please transfer at once."

Miss Pera Sotherton swallowed. "What about the others?"

The flaming badges of rank on the golden coveralls glittered as the Customs man regarded her.

"You wait. You may, if you wish, travel on to the next solar system. The choice is yours."

The young ship's officer from *Iquique* protested. "You know this shell couldn't make it. It only has Togossens. You'll have to evacuate the shell inside six hours before the systems run down anyway, and –"

"All H.G.L. out!" the customs man broke in, brutally
14

brushing past. He was doing his job; but Hook saw he enjoyed the doing of it and the manner of that doing. Hook marked him.

People employed by or members of Hardman Galactic Lines surged up from their seats and made for the air lock. Others, members of different econorgs, were pushed aside. As was to be expected aboard an H.G.L. ship the majority were travelling aboard a ship of their own conglomerate. When they had all left there were twenty people remaining.

Pera Sotherton said: "I work for Pattens. My boss was in such a hurry – I should never have come aboard this ship!"

The Customs man returned. Hook knew exactly what he was going to say.

"All those who can pay for transfer to planetary surface please pay now and take your seats in the tender."

Three chins wabbling, the wealthy woman gobbled her way to the airlock, her fists clutching money-metal. Hook took his eyes off her to see Pera Sotherton feverishly counting a few slips of money-metal she took from the waist-pouch of her glitter-gown. She counted twice and then counted again. "Five! That won't be enough. She started to rise.

Hook said: "That golden bastard is charging two thousand, Miss Sotherton."

"But I left my money in the ship's safe!"

"Too bad."

"And you?"

Hook flicked a pocket of his tunic open. "A ten and a five."

"So we can't – we can't get out of here –"

"They'll come up for us when they feel like it. If you're not a member of an econorg they recognise, or you can't pay –"

"I know. You don't have to rub it in."

Everyone knew. It was a fact of life in the galaxy of the hundred and first century.

Iquique's officer came back. He looked sick. Hook had to hand it to him for an organisation man; the kid had guts.

"I'm very sorry, taynors and tanisses. But as soon as I contact H.G.L. office, I shall –"

The bristle-haired Riffian shouted: "Can't you pilot this god-dammed shell down, youngster? Isn't that your job?"

15

The officer spread his hands. "I'm not a pilot, sir. These shells can be driven for planetfall; but it is not easy. It is dangerous, in fact – best to wait –"

"Goddamn you, and goddamn H.G.L.!"

Everyone who had a credit card with H.G.L. or an econorg represented on Lerdun below, or who could pay, left. Pera leaned back. Sweat slicked on her forehead. "We can only wait, then . . ."

Hook stood up. "I think," said Ryder Hook, "I am in no mood to wait."

CHAPTER TWO

H.G.L. STARSHIP *Iquique*'s life shell fled around the flank of the planet Lerdun. Lerdun was a free world. That, in the experience of Ryder Hook, might mean anything from an open planet for criminals to the tightest-mind-blocked religion-obsessed world. There was no norm in so profuse a galaxy of inhabited worlds; but again in Ryder Hook's experience some free worlds were the most pleasant on which to live. A single glance at the gold coveralled Customs man had told Hook that Lerdun could not be one of these.

Pera Sotherton said: "But – we'll have to wait, Mr. Hook."

They were on the mister and miss level, then, now. Nice.

"We jetted last from *Iquique*," Hook said. He spoke calmly but he did not stop walking up the central aisle past the rows of empty seats towards the control deck beyond the screen. "We picked up this world of Lerdun. It seems to me the other shells must have picked up an earlier bio-applicable planet. We're on our own, here."

He did not add that being on his own was familiar to him.

She trailed him up the aisle. The remaining passengers were reacting in different ways. A furry ovoid with a fungus-mop of hair and prehensile tail had curled himself up on a crystal tripod and his keening voice modulated intricate Tra'ailin scales as he strove in his way to accept the situation. A human with red hair and protruding eyes was methodically slamming his fist into the arm of his chair and letting rip a complicated string of obscenities culled from a hundred planets' cultures. The little furry Cailiang woman had gone. She belonged to Interstell-Imp who had an agency on Lerdun. Pera Sotherton followed Hook, and the bristled-haired Riffian, who owned to the name of Giffler, followed Pera.

These people left were only too well aware of the danger facing them. They had no protection from their own econorgs who were not represented on Lerdun, and they did not have enough money-metal to pay for passage down to the planet. That most of them had had money-metal safely stowed in *Iquique*'s safe meant nothing. Without a wrist credit card or money-metal, you were nothing in the galaxy.

Ryder Hook, sometimes known as Jack Kinch, did not have a wrist credit card of any description.

"Can you –?" Pera said, and hesitated.

"Yes," said Ryder Hook.

The red-haired terrestrial looked up at them and stopped slamming his fist into the arm of his chair. He swivelled his head to follow them. Then he jumped up and charged along the aisle, in the light artificial gravity floating over the plastic-runged metalloy floor, pushed past the Riffian, Giffler.

"Hey! What's going on here?"

Hook didn't bother to answer. He slid the partition open and stepped in. The control deck looked about as he expected. These life shells were produced as cheaply as possible. Once their sole function had been discharged they could be abandoned. Everyone devoutly wished that function never had to be discharged.

Hook settled himself into the pilot's throne and drew a lap punch-board across. He studied the layout.

He became aware of Pera Sotherton saying: "He's going to take us down, Taynor Dittrich."

"Like hell he is!"

The red-haired terrestrial who must be Dittrich pushed past and thrust his bulk onto the control deck. He shouted. He was clearly more scared than angry.

"Hey, you! Who says you're taking this shell down?"

Hook did not look up. He went on methodically punching out a preflight pattern. Everything had been built lightly and cheaply – it was not necessarily built simply, for that was a penalty of cheapness. Still, with a little luck he ought to bring the shell through atmosphere without a burn-up.

A hand fell on his shoulder, gripping through the dark grey tunic material.

"Listen, gonil! You're not risking my life in a flame-out! Get offa them controls!"

Pera tried to intervene; but Dittrich shoved her back. Giffler was frenziedly doing nothing in the background.

Many times in his life Ryder Hook had felt the grip of authority fall on his shoulder. When he could do nothing but accept that touch, he had done so; but with mental reservations that brooked ill for authority. When, as now, the man thus gripping him had no business doing so, Hook would not tolerate the indignity.

He reached up with his left hand, took Dittrich's arm in his fist, hauled the man down, turned his head away from him and lightly pressed the knuckle of his first finger behind the man's ear. He pushed the senseless man away and said: "Have Giffler help you take him back to a seat, Pera." He had used the minimum of movement and his voice remained as level and as unemotional as a man reading a video guide.

Pera put a hand to her lips, her eyes wide.

Giffler chuckled.

"Here, Tayniss Sotherton. Best do as this wild one asks."

Between them they dragged Dittrich out.

Hook returned his attention to the controls.

Wild one. Hell. Just how much of this mask of emotionless efficiency he adopted had the Riffian penetrated?

Ryder Hook held down a seething mass of emotions. He had been doing it for a long time and he intended to go on repressing his natural streak of savage barbarity; but he felt that he must have betrayed more than he expected to the Riffian. The old bristle-haired character saw a lot more than Hook had at first given him credit for through that transceiver mounted over his nose. Aliens, aliens . . . They were always providing the unexpected.

In the main passenger compartment of the life shell Giffler and Pera quietened down the rest of the people. Just what dangers were involved in putting a life shell down no one really understood. The shells were built to take survivors from a spacewreck and transport them as rapidly as possible to the nearest bio-applicable planet. After that, surface tenders would rise from the surface to make contact and transport the survivors to

19

safety. Sometimes, in certain circumstances, one of the limited-application transmats might be sent up and then the survivors could transmat to the surface without the discomforts of a bumpy ride. In the event that the bio-applicable planet selected had no intelligent occupants and the shell must extemporise some landing of its own, it was built to make a planetfall. Experienced pilots disliked the task. It could be done; no one would do it without good and sufficient reason.

Ryder Hook had no other reasons than his dislike of being pushed around and his conviction that these survivors with him would be left until very near the end, when the systems were failing to the point of extreme discomfort inboard, before the men from Lerdun would come up to get them. There were very good reasons for this. The Customs men would bleed them dry; after that, penniless, they would be fair prey to all the laws and rapacious overlords Hook knew – by experience for he had never visited Lerdun previously – to exist on the planet below.

By the time Giffler put his transceiver-bridged nose back into the control compartment Hook was ready.

"You can –" began Giffler. Then he stopped speaking. Old he might be, more fragile than he used to be; but Giffler of Riffia – a hard-headed lot in the galaxy – knew what he knew about men. He knew, now, that if anyone could land them safely on planet, this man Ryder Hook could. Giffler understood only too well the disasters they would suffer if they remained and suffered in orbit and waited to be bled dry by the Lerduns.

Ryder Hook looked up.

"Everyone will have to strap in. It will be a bumpy road."

Pera Sotherton made a face; she was uncomfortably aware that she was not at all afraid in a situation that should be driving her into the shiver-and-shakes of total fright. She shot a glance at Ryder Hook. Goddamn him for a conniving male animal if he was having this soothing effect on her!

Hook settled, checked the readouts, completed the pre-flight pattern. He selected an area the bio-scanner told him was in the high-acceptance ratio. He did not wish to land in a desert, or in the oceans of this world. Finally, with everything set to go, he punched the retro-circuit button and felt the deceleration effects shiver up through his spine.

"Finagling layabouts," he said to himself. It was perfectly safe to talk to himself for the neural net to any of those controls within range – there were probably at least half a dozen, and more probably ten, who would come on net if he charged out their call – was most positively switched off. He was now referring to the financial wizards who had outlined the parameters and the specs for *Iquique*'s life shells. As the mild deceleration came on and the shell nosed out of orbit, Hook reflected on the pleasant prospect of having to ride the shell all the way down. It had been equipped with rockets – plastic-solid fuel permanently sealed and safe from deterioration fuelled the jets – so there would be no easy connection with ground control and a tight beam-ride-in on engines that seized the indestructible fabric of space-time itself and twisted themselves along between the stars. Ride cheap, survive dear.

The shell dropped for atmosphere.

Hook sat blockily in the throne and watched tell-tales. Thermocouples began to agitate. He just hoped the foxey builders of the shell hadn't skimped on hull insulation. The whole shebang might come apart as atmospheric friction sought to burn it out of the sky.

The shell dived planetwards. Hook was not going for a glance and a bounce out into space, for he had no excess of speed to dissipate. This would be a simple ride-in like they used to do in the old days before spatial engines had been developed to obviate all this rocket and atmosphere friction and judgements of approach nonsense. His brown eyes brooded on the tell tales. His hands poised above the controls. He could feel deceleration coming on, gently at first, building, building . . .

Probe signals combed the surface and relayed information on contours and surfaces back to the outputs on the console. He had some measure of guidance left before they entered the chute and he selected an area that appeared, as far as he could judge, to be as flat as any. The shell began to vibrate. Now they were plunging through the tenuous outer wisps of atmosphere. Thermocouples and stress meters told the story of mounting resistance outside, of mounting pressure and temperature and strain. Hook let his senses meld and slide and flow into the complex of

the shell so that he became an extension of the mechanical arti-
fact.

Deceleration pressed him deeply into the sprung throne. That
special project he had been asked to join that had caused all his
woes in the galaxy certainly paid a handsome dividend now. In
a situation where a normal man would have difficulty in lifting
his head, Hook could sit normally relaxed in the throne and use
his body as though he moved under one gee.

A voice croaked through on the intercomm.

"You – all – right – up front?"

"Perfectly, thank you, Taynor Giffler. May I suggest you re-
serve your strength?"

"You – may."

Hook seldom smiled – he had little in life to smile about – but
he enjoyed a good liberating belly-laugh. He felt a small inner
amusement that his mild words might throw a little more dust
in Giffler's transceiver.

The shell screamed through air. Its hull began to heat up and
the heat-sink smoked and flamed and the whole craft plummeted
groundwards enveloped in a fireball and trailing a streamer of
flame.

Hook looked at the fuel gauges and once again he said: "The
penny-pinching bastards."

There was fuel enough to allow him one braking pass. If he
fouled up the first time all the fuel would have been spent and
he would have no power to prevent the shell from smashing into
the ground. Nice. A situation so un-novel for Ryder Hook that
he calculated it into his life-pattern as just another problem. But
it was nice to have a good cuss at the H.G.L. moguls who had
decided this set-up was good enough for their passengers.

Shaped something like a shoe the life shell possessed two
stumpy wings that had been extended during the pre-flighting.
Hook felt the snapping vibration and the crazy rolling. His
hands flew above the controls, expending fractional amounts of
fuel to correct the plunge. He retracted the remaining wing. The
other one had burned clean through, snapping off like heated
toffee stringing and solidifying and twisting. The shell lurched
and backed and heat began to smash in solid waves through the
hull. Hook dragged the thing back into the chute by movements

fast and precise and by taking his fuel level down to the danger-line.

He'd lost a wing; the other was retracted. He was going in on his belly, sliding the shell through atmosphere like a stone skipping water. What a hell of a mess!

The heat built up and sweat rolled down his chest. The shell was going mad and the telltales relayed that story. The shell had lost a wing and retracted the other. No shell could come in without some aerodynamic assist. Hook felt his face writhing into a grimace he knew from old was a ghastly snarl, a barbarically savage challenge to all the god-forsaken laws of nature and the cold arbiters of the universe. He cursed the laws of astrophysics!

He was going to bring this shell in, if it killed him.

He eased up in the chute to the very limit of tolerance. The passengers must have given up hope now. They must be sweating and praying and screaming. He had to subject them to this torture to take the knots off the shell. Once he was down to a manageable speed he could control it in himself; but he had to *fly* the damn thing in!

No man whose body structure and muscles had not been subjected to the severe conditioning Hook had received as a young volunteer on RCI's Powerman Project could have done what he was doing now. As the shell flamed earthwards and the telltales screamed their warnings and the probe picked out possible landing sites, Hook was able to manipulate controls and fly the life shell as though riding a disintegrating comet.

He felt every bump and shock through the seat of his pants. Bits of insulation packing fell from the overhead. Some wiring was burning somewhere and stinking blue smoke puffed and fled into the gobbling maw of the air conditioner. The shell shook. It danced and skated through the air.

By the time the thicker levels came up most of the forward portions had melted and flowed away. Just how long the heat shield would hold Hook could only guess. If that went no amount of Powerman procedures could stop him from being fried.

If the forward tubes went also – then no one aboard had the slightest hope.

They would just plunge down and smash scorchingly into

23

the ground like a meteor gone mad. They'd blow a hole you could drop a city block into and no one would notice the tv aerials atop the spire.

Now the heat pouring into the back of the throne made his whole body ache and throb. Sweat rolled off him in gobbetts. He licked dry lips. He damned those finagling bastards at H.G.L. – and those heartless goons of Lerdun. But for them this would not have been necessary.

He caught a scathing glimpse of fire streaking past the tiny observation window above his head. It was pitted with darker streaks as the whole forward end of the craft melted and crumbled away.

The body of the shell received enough protection to remain habitable. That might not last much longer.

He had to calculate out the exactly right time to fire the retros. Once they'd fired he'd be drained of fuel. Too high – and velocity would build up again too early. Too low – and they wouldn't brake in time.

He studied the screen before him. So far the camera lenses were still intact, although hazed and rimed with the fire that lacerated them. He could see clouds, and the glitter of a river, and a scattering of mountains that vanished off the screen as he watched. He could estimate height and confirm by the terrestrial altimeter. He'd go by the soles of his feet on that one, would Ryder Hook, and use the instrument merely as a confirmatory device.

In an incandescent streak of flame the shell scorched across the sky.

Hook fired his forward tubes and the retros splashed fresh flame into the inferno.

He extended his brakes and felt the craft juddering and shaking. A tell-tale panel blew in a gout of smoke. The whole thing was shaking and shuddering and dancing. He held onto the controls and pulled her slowly up. She flattened. Now the shell had become a live thing struggling to survive, to pitch them back into space, to bounce them away from the cold ground of Lerdun. Hook held her to it and took the shell in along the terminal path of the chute approach.

The shell broke up.

An enormous boot drove upwards sledging into Ryder Hook's back. He cursed some more but held on.

The shell broke up.

Shedding bits and pieces it skidded across a dusty plain, smashing down trees, ripping portions of metalloy away on rocks and gullies, driving on and on, smashing and rending and tearing, collapsing, coming to rest at last, a smoking heap of mangled wreckage.

The shell was on fire and smoke stank into the air.

Hook unstrapped and levered himself up.

Damn all the moguls of space! He'd brought her in.

They were down.

CHAPTER THREE

"THEY'LL have been watching us," said Ryder Hook. "They know we're here. They won't be long."

Miraculously enough no one had been killed in that brutal landing. Giffler wheezed a little, getting his breath, and Dittrich showed signs of wanting to bash Hook in the guts. The other passengers were only too relieved to be down onplanet in one piece.

Pera Sotherton scanned the sky. They had recovered now, and a couple of hours had gone by. Those were terrestrial hours, of course, for her and Hook, although the time-pieces of the other humanoids and aliens might operate with hours of any length the solar systems of the galaxy cared. Now Pera pointed.

"There they are."

The high remote glitter of a flier canopy speared a glint of reflected sunlight. Hook looked away. Around them stretched the dusty plain, with a few hills ringing the northern horizon. A road of reasonable construction ran east-west and away to the south the hint of a forest pushed a scrap of welcome greenness into the prevailing grey and ochre. He'd picked a good site to come down in.

The flier circled once and then slanted in for a touchdown.

The survivors all bedraggled and bruised and dishevelled waited for the men from Lerdun to walk across to them.

Thoughts could run deep in Ryder Hook and just now he was aware of his own introspection; given the kind of life he was now forced to lead because of those bastards at RCI and their womb-regurgitants of Boosted Men there came few moments when he could allow himself to be off guard. He could think of a number of highly imaginative concepts as these golden-coveralled Customs Men of Lerdun walked across from their flier, see the whole situation in terms of psychological cross-currents and mutual hatreds and fears and passions. As it was he stood there, balanced evenly, his arms hanging at his sides, yet he was ready to take off instantly and move like a hunting wild-cat.

Many men and women and aliens had tried to take advantage of Hook and most of them had just lived long enough to regret that disastrous miscalculation.

"We never thought you'd make it," said the Customs Man.

He was the same one.

The sun shot sparks from his collar and cuff insignia. He thought a great deal of himself, that was for sure.

"We need help —" Dittrich started, moving forward, holding out his hand.

"Of course, of course," said the Customs Man. "But you were not invited to land on our planet."

"What choice did we have?" Dittrich's hands shook.

"You chose to break your orbit and land here. We would have come up for you."

"Sure," said Giffler, moving forward, adjusting his nose-mounted transceiver. "When it suited you. When we'd been —"

"I think there has been enough of this petty wrangling." The man who spoke moved with a kind of sidling motion most disagreeable to Hook. He wore a dark tunic and breeches, in contrast to the others' golden coveralls, and his hair had been brushed stiffly back to stand in a white halo. White hair must be some kind of genetic defect, or affectation. These days men kept their hair intact and fully-coloured for eighty years at least. This man's face bore the kind of smile Hook had seen on the leading barracuda as it closed in, grinning, on its hunk of bloody meat.

To this man, Hook knew because he had met his like before, these survivors were simply hunks of meat, hung out bloodily to appease his appetites.

Just as Hook was trying to imagine what prayers this man's mother had taught him at her knee, Pera said in a breathy whisper: "But what are you going to *do*?"

The six men in golden coveralls, each with a lesser amount of flashiness about their insignia, moved out into a curved line facing the survivors. The Customs Man and the man in black remained in the centre of the line. There was the answer to Pera's question.

An alien from the Joyfarlan Cluster among the survivors shouted in a high shocked voice. "What –?"

The man in black said: "I am Goton Telander. You have chosen to land on our planet without invitation and without being represented here by any agency. There are certain formalities to be observed."

"Formalities!" shouted the alien from Joyfarlan, a being rotund as a beer barrel with six skimpy tendrils for hair and six skinny tendrils for arms and six fragile tendrils for legs. "Formalities! We have the rights of spacewrecked –"

"No." Goton Telander's voice slid softly but cuttingly, as cold as a mountain tarn. "No, you have no rights at all. You must pay landing fees, berthing tolls, aliens' permits and residents' permits. If you cannot pay the full amount you will work off the payments."

Hook had heard all this before.

"But our money was aboard *Iquique*!" said Pera.

"That is no concern to the authorities of Lerdun. Pay or enroll for repayments of out-loans made to you."

"Outloans?"

"You must pay to land on Lerdun. We are an open planet. If you cannot pay we can loan you the money-metal which you must then repay. The only way you can do that is to enrol as a covenanted labour-unit –"

Hook said: "You mean slave, don't you?"

Goton Telander reacted with the habitual grace of the man of power dealing with offensive underlings. He swivelled his lean head and stared down his nose at Hook. He took stock of the man.

"We are a civilised planet, taynor. We do not employ slaves. We deplore the use of slave labour in the galaxy. You will merely sign as a covenanted labour-unit and work off the loan that has been made to you."

"So we've already contracted the loan?"

"Of course. You are here, are you not, uninvited, on the sacred soil of Lerdun?"

There was no answer to that.

28

This could not be the first time the Customs Man and his civil servant superior, Telander, had met people landing uninvited. They had their rules and their laws and they would enforce them. The six golden-coveralled men waiting so alertly were the enforcers. The planet ran its own government and as an open planet that government would be powerful and not weakened by the multi-system conglomerates and the econorgs. Here, on Lerdun, the conglomerates did what the government wanted out in the open, and under cover they would corrupt individuals of that government to see the world went the way they wanted.

"Take your seats in the flier." The Customs Man began to shepherd the survivors about, like a golden retriever worrying sheep.

Hook let his gaze dwell for an instant only on the surrounding plain. It had been a fine place to make an emergency landing in a life shell shot to pieces; but it was inhospitable. He ducked his head and entered the flier. There was little point in attacking this man out here.

The flier was slightly cramped with the number of survivors but no one took much notice of that and the journey to Lacan, the chief city hereabouts, took little time. They were decanted in the stone courtyard walled by plastic panels of the local Customs House where their particulars would be taken down – and Hook knew that the joke could be figurative or literal – ready for processing through to covenanted labour-units.

Slaves.

Hook never truly enjoyed being a slave.

You could still find idiots who thought slavery was a fine institution; but Hook, with his rapacious determination for perfection and efficiency, had proved to his own satisfaction that slavery was not efficient. Now, if he, Ryder Hook, was put in charge of an operation to make slavery really efficient ... H'mm – that might prove a challenge.

"Roust! Roust!" More golden-coveralled men appeared. They shepherded the survivors into lines and the processing began.

The processing took the form of relieving the survivors of all their money-metal and any other possessions of value still with them. If the total did not meet the dues, then automatic labour for determined periods would follow.

29

Dittrich protested.

"You can't do this to me! I'm with Sieur-Stel! That's a big conglomerate – better than a hundred systems in total control and agencies all over –"

"Not on Lerdun, gonil. Keep quiet." The Customs Man sauntered over, his hands hooked in his belt, superintending his men at their processing.

"But I'm a systems staffer! I demand you call the nearest Sieur-Stel agency –"

The Customs Man struck Dittrich across the face. He struck back-handedly, as though both contemptuous of the terrestrial bravura and ashamed at soiling his hand. Dittrich span backwards and fell. He clawed up wildly, a thread of scarlet splitting from his lower lip.

"You bastard! I know your game! You need slaves – you don't care for –"

The Customs Man kicked gently at Dittrich. Dittrich screamed all the same.

The Customs Man said: "Get this whoreson on his feet and processed. Then get him out of my sight."

His men jumped to obey.

Pera said: "Oh! The poor man!"

Hook had little sympathy for Dittrich.

"Roust!" shouted the Customs guards, herding them on.

The lines moved up. The tables for processing had been set up in a side doorway, one each side, and the familiar litter of ink-stamps, micro-readers, infra- and ultra-detectors lay scattered on their green plastic. Now Giffler pushed one thin arm into the micro-reader and twisted so that his wrist credit card presented its face to the reader.

"Don't waste my time!" said the processor. His eyes showed fatigue and he chewed stim-gum continuously, food spots stained the front of his golden coverall. "Get your money out!"

"I have only these three ones," said Giffler. His transceiver caught the last beams of sunlight over the plastic wall and flamed a glittering reflection. "I am quite certain if you call the Riffian embassy on Shatterway they will –"

"I said don't waste my time!" The processer looked up at the

Customs Man who sauntered across from the other table. Dittrich was being hauled off, yelling.

"Shatterway?" said the Customs Man. He smiled. "I do not like the people on Shatterway at all." Shatterway had been H.G.L. starship *Iquique*'s last port of call. He looked at Giffler's bridge-mounted transceiver. "Get that gadget off!"

Absolute panic hit Giffler.

"No! No, you can't! I'm blind and deaf – without my transceiver I'm helpless – you can't remove it!"

The lenses and sensors glittered in the last of the sunlight.

"Can't? There's nothing I can't do to you."

Giffler put a hand to his face and clutched the transceiver. He was shaking and shuddering as the life shell had trembled under enormous pressures.

This was no business of Hook's.

Just why he stuck his nose in, Ryder Hook could not be sure. Even as he spoke he was aware of just what kind of a fool he was being.

"If you take his transceiver he'll be blind and deaf and consequently of no use as a covenanted labour-unit."

The Customs Man did not turn. He simply lashed out with his hand, as he had with Dittrich, backhanded, to slap this troublesome Terran back.

Hook swayed aside and the blow hissed past.

"Look," said Ryder Hook, reasonably. "Let's be sensible about this."

He knew, now, why he was talking like a poltroon. But he had started and he wouldn't stop for this golden-coveralled buffoon, for all the power the man wielded at this minute.

Giffler shrieked as a guard came across and reached for the transceiver. The Customs Man recovered his balance and, with the speed of a striking sex-crazed strooka, drew his weapon. The Tonota Eighty could vapourise a man's head at six hundred metres.

A confusion followed. Giffler's crimson shoulder-cloak flared and vanished in a gout of flame. The guard reeled back.

"Curd!" yelled the processor and heaved up oversetting his table. Hook lay on the ground, feeling his head gonging from a second guard's blow. The Customs men were running.

31

And Giffler —

Someone had used a Delling on him.

Pera Sotherton, her hands over her face, was screaming and screaming . . .

Giffler melted.

His body deliquesced. It oozed. His head flowed and collapsed and sloughed. Still upright, he melted and shrank and collapsed, his body shimmered like a blood-drenched jelly. He shrank and oozed and formed a contracting pool of scum on the yard stones.

Hook climbed slowly to his feet.

The man in black, Goton Telander, walked out of the Custom House door. He still held the Delling. With a finicky motion he flicked his fingers and the electronic and neural circuits whipped the gun back up his sleeve. It had all been so very slow and yet so very quick.

Giffler had been destroyed.

Hook put a hand on Pera's shoulder and squeezed. She stopped screaming and gasped and then she began to sob.

A robot vacuum cleaner and scrubber darted out on rubber wheels and began to suck and clean the spot where Giffler had died.

CHAPTER IV

LACAN, as a city, had not impressed Hook from what little he had seen of it coming in in the flier. Functional, with grouped building-complexes, served by flyovers and automated tread-ways, pitted with parks and lakes, dotted with trees and that pec-uliarly lovely fire-bush from Ronan IV, the love-shrub, the city nevertheless failed to integrate into a livable whole. Hook, pen-ned between plastic walls and the Custom House, watching a robot cleaner trundle away bearing the last few atoms of Giffler, was in no position to make finicky judgements about this city.

Pera was next in line.

Hook gave her a tiny push forward, a gentle urge to straighten her up. The emotion of pity came rarely to him, inured as he was to scenes of horror and terror, and with a background of personal tragedy. He was no superman. He had to remember that. Oh, those monkeys at RCI had played around with the atoms and molecules of his cells, given his proteins metallic bases, turned his bones into semi-metallic constructs that could withstand titanic gee forces, as he had found so useful when *Iquique* blew. He had organic implants in his skull through which, purely by scientific and electronic means he could go on net to control many parsecs away across the interstellar gulfs. He could do many things that a normal man could not do; but he was not, he most certainly was not, a superman.

Had he been a superman – or had a Boosted Man happened by – Hook might have acted differently from the way he did act.

He hadn't known a person called Giffler existed before *Iquique*. He hadn't considered the whirlpool of stars held a girl like Pera Sotherton. He was not fool enough to think he might fall in love with her; that kind of love was not reserved for him.

33

There were ten customs men in the yard. There were two processors sitting behind their tables. The stim-gum chewing processor had righted his table and re-arranged his paraphernalia and was now awaiting Pera Sotherton. The Customs Man stalked back and forth, left hand resting on his gunbutt. Goton Telander watched the scene with that remote and crafty look on his face that Hook had seen on the faces of Werkler cats after they had eaten Werkler mice.

Well – it might as well be now as later.

The other processor shouted: "You! Plug-ugly! Roust! C'mere!"

Obediently Hook walked across to the other table. The processor, a large individual with a paunch kept in place by a stasisbelt, grunted and stabbed a finger at Hook.

"Get your money-metal on the table, gonil! Let's see your wrist credit-card."

Hook put his five and his ten on the table.

"I don't have a credit card."

The processor didn't look up. His voice thickened.

"Quit the clowning! Let's see." He grabbed for Hook's left hand. He found it well-nigh impossible to imagine a man who could travel by starship would not possess a credit card, be a part of the galaxy-spanning conglomerate system, be an organisation man.

"Here," said Ryder Hook. "Look."

He thrust out his left arm.

The processor's hand missed its mark. Hook's arm went on. The fingers doubled up into a fist, an exceedingly hard fist. That fist smashed into the processor's face and cracked his nose. Before he had time to shriek, before he had time to topple backwards, Hook was over the table in a running dive, had scooped up the fellow's gun from its holster and was flattening out against the wall. The gun was a Swan-Durk magnum. Hook shot the Customs Man. He hit the guy in the middle of his belly and sprayed guts and blood six feet past him. The Swan-Durk held ten rounds. By the time Hook finished shooting only one Customs man was on his feet, glaring around wildly with his gun in his fist and spattered remains from a companion slick on his hair and cheek. Hook had been moving. He had not re-

34

mained still to shoot; but he had shot and moved, shot and moved. The wall at the processor's back was fused and burned and chipped and both processors were dead, cut down by Customs men.

Hook leaped for the remaining guard, chopped him across the neck, twisted his gun away and shot him before he hit the stone yard.

Goton Telander had vanished.

Little time had elapsed.

"You can go where you like," Hook said to the dazed survivors. He gestured to the closed gate. "I'd suggest you didn't go into the Customs House. You can stay here if you want to be slaves."

He ran for the gate, the gun big and bulky in his fist.

Pera Sotherton screeched and fled over the stones. She caught him as he swung the gate open.

"I'm coming! You can't leave me behind."

Hook spared her a dispassionate glance.

"I can," he said. "Don't make that mistake. If you come with me you take your own chances."

"I will, I will! Only, for Great Salvor's sake, let's get out of here."

Hook shoved the gate open just enough for them both to slip through and they lifted their feet and ran.

The streets were lit pallidly and coldly by spaced arcs.

Few people were about, and a drifting of silent electric traffic along the boulevards. In an hour or so, surmised Hook, the place would pick up. At the moment folk were at home eating their evening meal. The city was small enough and functional enough to contain an almost village culture.

"Where are we going, Mr. Hook?"

He didn't bother to answer.

Even if he knew the answer, he wouldn't have wasted breath on a reply.

He padded on. He thrust the gun into the waistband of his pants. The dark blue tunic blended well; it was a standard interstellar type and cut garment, anyway. Pera's own silvery glitter-gown, ripped and torn, would draw eyes.

35

He said: "If you intend to stay with me you'll have to find less conspicuous clothes."

He didn't wait for her reply but kept on going.

They passed a corner anti-grav shaft leading to the annex of a subterranean complex servicing the city. Hook gave it a cool appraising glance that took in the dangers that might be expected from the black shaft mouth, with its circle of low-wattage bulbs. He had no intention of using it. The first place the Lerdun enforcers would look for them would be in the service channels and underground tunnels. The sky opened up at their backs with the yammer – an irritating sound, that yammer, designed to fibrillate the nerves – of a warning siren.

"That's the signal," panted Pera, struggling on to keep up with Hook. "They know we've escaped."

"Let's hope they take off after some of the others, then."

"You're a callous bastard, Hook, aren't you?"

"No. Realistic."

He started diagonally across the roadway, jumping the moving slats of the treadwalk.

"There's a store over there."

"So what good is a store?" She caught up with him and halted, getting her breath, staring in at the displayed clothes behind the armour-glass. "We've no money."

Hook lifted the big Tonota Eighty and melted down the armour-glass. A burglar alarm began to wail.

"Grab a tunic and pants, sombre colours, undistinguished. Hurry."

Pera fought down the panic fluttering in her stomach. This ugly brute Hook could chill her with revulsion. Also, she admitted, swiftly selecting a likely-looking set of clothing, he indisputably contained a feral power and primitive charm. For example, melting down a store window and stealing clothes. Would a normal man do that?

Hook caught something of her feelings. Despite his own intolerance of other people, he said: "Every man and woman and humanoid must be regarded as being against us, Pera. It isn't nice. I don't enjoy destruction. But I don't intend to be killed or enslaved."

She stripped the glitter dress off, bundling it up and then

looking about helplessly. She wore flame-red pants and breast cups. Hook took the glitter-gown and tossed it into the shop.

As Pera stuck one leg into the pants Hook burned the shop with two swift blasts from the Tonota. The store belched flames.

"Maybe they might think twice, after this," said Ryder Hook.

He took no satisfaction from wanton destruction. But, this burning concealed tracks. Long before the forensic people got their detectors to sniff out the body-odours and skin and hair particles from himself and Pera trapped here he'd be gone. If the girl stayed with him, all right. He had found a use for her that he would introduce later and let her suggest.

They padded up the road. Hook wondered how long it would take her to come up with the obvious solution to their problems.

She seemed a nice bright kid. She must have a decent job to be travelling in style aboard *Iquique*. Many and many a time Hook had travelled between the stars low style, frozen like a side of beef. He didn't like doing that. No one did. There was a higher risk of never coming out of the stasis than there was of being mis-routed over the transmat.

"But, Hook, what are we going to *do*?"

"Get our heads down. I'm hungry. Those rations aboard the life shell did nothing for my metabolism."

"Hungry! You can think of your stomach at a time like this?"

"It's always a time like this. Stomachs are very important."

Pera thought of the Customs Man and the way he had been parted from his stomach, and she shuddered. She had been used to a quiet job as secretary to old man Porten, working for Pattens, a pretty important multi-system conglomerate. Desks and inter-office communication devices and agendas and routine and coffee breaks; they had made up her life so far. That life against which she had so often railed when all the galaxy glittered and beckoned to her she now looked back on with a pungent nostalgic pang, the feeling she would never get back to normalcy. Ryder Hook, she was certain, was not normal.

But, then, in the situation they were now in with every person's hand turned against them, normalcy was of little use.

A man like Ryder Hook meant survival.

The big Tonota Eighty went back down Hook's waistband. He dragged a flap of his tunic up and covered the butt; but the gun was difficult to hide. Lots of men and aliens preferred the feel of a big gun in their fist rather than a nifty electronic and neural system that could slap a gun out from under your sleeve faster than a man could draw. It was all old stuff now; Hook didn't care what weapon he used provided he got the other guy first and stayed alive.

The irritating yammering of the alarms floated annoyingly over the city. Hook decided he didn't like this dump called Lacan one little bit. At that, if he could find a more modern city he could nudge Pera into suggesting the obvious.

They stepped onto a treadwalk and the slats whisked them along at a brisk walking pace. A few other people were appearing now and an alien – a cheerful creature from Narses with a bright yellow face and facial whiskers half a metre long – stared at them comically. Hook moved up to Pera and put a hand around her waist.

He did something with his lips that might have passed as a smile and nodded to the Narsian.

The long whiskers lifted in a grimace that resembled a return smile and the cheerful alien waddled off, his bushy tail waggling.

"They'll find us soon, Hook, and then we'll –"

"Just shut up and cuddle up. This is evening boulevard time on this bloody planet, unless I miss my bet."

"You don't like people, do you, Hook? And yet – yet you waited until they killed Giffler before –"

"What I do is my business. Giffler meant nothing to me. Of course I don't like people. Since when have people ever done me any good?"

"You're a right chancroid, aren't you?"

"Sure," said Hook, who had been called so many filthy names in his time he ought to have kept a lexicon of them and published it to educate schoolkids.

She tried to twist free of his arm; but Hook kept her firmly anchored.

"What do you know of this lousy planet and this city, Pera?"

She left off struggling and let out a gasp of anger. "Oh, you –! Not much. It's lousy, like you said. We don't have an agency here. What Mr. Porten would say, I don't know."

"Porten the big boss?"

"Mister Porten is an important man in Patten's. He's tenth vice-president and in charge of systems control."

"Is he now."

Hook had weighed the chances of calling out to a control net and decided against them. His organic wiring was good, he knew that. He could probably cut into any number of nets if he chose. But he had the uneasy suspicion that the Boosted Men had been breathing down his back the last time. He'd have to let Pera suggest the solution herself. If she left it too late he'd show her. He ought to be skilful enough for that, God knew; but – but he felt that in some obscure way she would suspect a trick if he came right out and told her what they ought to do.

Mind you, she'd be right.

She was still partially shocked by what had happened. Hook could see clearly enough that this kind of carry-on was right outside her range of experience. What sort of chance would she have stood as an indentured slave – a covenanted labour-unit?

"What else do you know? Any modern cities about?"

"Of course. Lerdun is a primary planet, it evolved its own culture and was not colonised. I have a vague impression the capital city is down south – oh, Hook! Why don't you plug into an outlet and dial information?"

Hook realised with pleasure that her exclamation and use of his name came from exasperation. Plugging into an outlet and asking questions were the normal methods, ones he would have used without thinking in other circumstances. Still ... He might just get away with it, even now. If he was quick.

"All right, Pera. We'll just do that."

The telephone booth he selected snugged against a plastic orange-coloured wall concealing a department store with its robots and its passing display of merchandise, all situated under a sports-drome and arena. The restaurants and bars up there were slowly filling under the evening's illuminations and soon the usual nightly hunting after pleasure would take over. Finding pleasure of one form or another was one of the most powerful motive forces in the galaxy. As it should be, Hook supposed, with a sigh he didn't fully comprehend, as it should be.

"Oh!" said Pera as the phone booth door hissed shut on ram-air. This time her exclamation was of dismay. "We don't have any money!"

"You'll start thinking again, soon, Pera. When you do hold onto this. If you spit in the galaxy's eye and duck, you'll do all right."

"So how do we dial out without cash or credits?"

"Like this."

Hook flicked his knife into his fingers, unscrewed the control console side and eased the plastic slab down. He looked at the circuitry inside for a moment, visualising. If any tenth-rate electronics man couldn't fix a tel-booth inside thirty seconds he'd be drummed out of the union. Hook reached in and began to rearrange terminals. He wasn't tenth rate – at least he kidded himself he wasn't – and although he was a jack of all trades in the galaxy, he had enough remnants of pride left him to know that did not mean he was master of none.

The screen lit and a pleasantly modulated voice said: "What service do you require, please?"

"Planetary information."

A dun-coloured patrol car whistled past outside on the street, sirening electric buggies out of its way, its orange flasher going like a one-eyed demon's eye with a severe tic.

"Planetary info," a second beautifully-modulated voice said. These were pre-recorded voices on tapes, served up to purpose from the planet's central computer. Hook had linked in with a little fiddle with the circuits; but he was well aware that he had perhaps thirty seconds to collect the data he needed.

"List modern cities."

The list came on. Lacan was around two-thirds of the way down the list.

"That's the capital," said Pera, pointing to the first name.

Hook selected a name a third of the way down and said: "Cantacle."

Instantly a street-map appeared and, subjoined, a list of flier and ground connections. Hook grunted and stored the information away. Then, at random he spoke up four more names and had their info pasted up across the screen.

"Is all," he said, finally. And, to Pera: "Come on, girl. Run!"

They bolted out of the phone booth and hared away up the

40

street, angling away from the orange wall. At the top corner Hook paused and looked back. Forty-five seconds. The planetary goons were slow around here. He slowed to a walk and rounded the pillar of an overhead archway carrying live-ware and heard the punching shock of the explosion. He looked back.

The phone booth collapsed into a deliquescing puddle of plastic and metal. The flier shot vengefully past and put another burst into the mess, just to make sure.

"Too late, you bastards," said Ryder Hook – and chuckled.

CHAPTER FIVE

AT the metalloy entrance gates to the flier park Pera Sotherton hung back. Her face showed lines where lines had no business to be. "They'll have homotropic stuff, Hook."

"Of course." He looked down on her. Poor kid, she just wasn't used to this kind of situation at all. "Their sniffers would have found us long ago if –" He paused. Why should he tell her that he'd a dinky little homo-tropic fouler-upper embedded in his skull along with all the other gadgets? He went on: "I managed to buy a homotropic double heterodyne from old Filker Fredericks, oh, way back when. Just pray it holds out."

"I will," she said, and let go his arm as he produced the Tonota Eighty and blew the gate-lock off.

"Someone will be along in no time at all. Run, Pera."

Homotropic devices would be monitoring the flier park just as they monitored any site where thieves or vandals or just plain idiots might break in and cause damage. They fastened their electronic feelers on a guy's brain-wave patterns and sweat-emissions and breathing and heart-rhythms, scenting human life – or alien life, of course – at a distance. The more credits you paid for your homotropic device the greater the sophistication and range you bought.

A flier park ought to have gear able to pick up a prowler at half a mile. Hook shoved Pera on and angled her towards the flier he had selected. The park was about half-full, and more fliers could be expected to arrive momentarily, as the attendants would say. The little craft sat in their neat rows, all makes and sizes, including plenty of off-planet models, indication that Lerdun was not a poor planet. Hook chose a neat little four-place job, a DM Tornado, coloured a glittery-blue and flicked open

42

the canopy with the edge of his knife. The broken catch glittered in the arc lights.

The alarm siren began at once, keyed as it was to every safety device on every flier in the park.

"Oh, dammit!" panted Pera.

Hook thought she was referring to the siren. "We'll be gone before they react —"

"No, you great clunkhead! I've caught my pants!"

Hook reached down and yanked her up. He hauled her by the armpit. She squealed. There was a ripping sound. A sizeable portion of flame briefs showed through the rent in the stolen pants.

Hook chuckled again. He was quite enjoying himself. "You never made your clothes allowance budget, I'll bet."

"Clothes allowance!" Pera sniffed. "How ancient can you get?"

The Tornado's lock yielded to Hook's expertly illegal ministrations and he took the craft up on her anti gravs with a single fluid motion. He wanted to get up and then, immediately, get *down.*

Pera gasped as the flier plunged for the main east-west boulevard, skating out over the pedestrians and ground cars. The automatic blast almost got them, at that. They felt the heat scorch in through the rear canopy. Then Hook savaged the controls and the flier responded and zoomed away over the roofs of Lacan. In mere seconds they had dropped the place beyond the horizon.

"And," said Ryder Hook, "that is a satisfactory place for it to be. Now perhaps we can get on with what we set out to do."

"Huh," said Pera. "For me, that was going to Albeira."

Hook felt some satisfaction. The girl was responding more like a human being and less like a tingirl robot. They sped through the night and as the artificial lights dropped away astern so the stars of the galaxy blazed out above them. People of the hundred and first century could look up at the stars and see them, not as mere twinkling dots of light in the night sky, but as destinations.

Hook had once had the horrors after a nightmare in which he had dreamed he belonged to a civilisation which had not devel-

43

oped interstellar travel, and was thereby bound and confined to its own solar system. That, to a man like Hook, was claustrophobia of the most horrific kind.

He had to get offplanet. He had no money, no credit card, no assistance of any sort – apart from what he could cajole from Pera Sotherton.

He had been in this situation before and, given the circumstances of his erratic life, would be again. He would so get offplanet. At least, the means of getting off existed. Starships waited for passengers at spaceports around this world. To be down on a planet which had no starships, no vessels that could take the indestructible fabric of space-time and twirl it around and so cross the great gulfs at speeds that gave a human's lifespan meaning, to be down on such a world was the ever-waiting nightmare for a galactic adventurer.

"Do you think they'll be fooled by your asking for the other cities from information?"

"No," said Hook. "But they'll check them all out. That should give us time."

If, Ryder Hook vowed, if she said: "Time to do what?" he'd put the flier on auto, put her over his knees, and spank that flame-pantied bottom. She must think of the obvious soon. Time was running out too fast. He stuck to his resolution, and did not urge her along. It was staring her in the face, after all . . .

This planet of Lerdun was an open world. It had a minimal central government, heavily staffed with enforcers, and it welcomed agencies of the many multi-system conglomerates. Everything had a price tag. Lerdun was a rich world and there were pickings for those in the know, those ruthless enough to go out and get what they wanted, the clever ones. For those with the right connections this world could be paradise.

For the loner this world was a death trap.

Ryder Hook was a loner. If he was in a death trap he'd damn well see a lot more deaths took place before his own.

Equally, although Lerdun welcomed the agencies of the galaxy's many econorgs, if an econorg was not represented, then that conglomerate would find it hard to get a toehold now all the richest plums had been picked. Pattens, for whom Pera worked, stood no chance at all of breaking in.

44

No chance, that is, with the set-up as it existed now.

"Cantacle is coming up inside the hour, Hook."

"Just hope it is modern, Pera."

"That info list said Lacan was modern."

"Well, hope harder."

Mind you, the term modern meant different things on different planets. In a frontier planet of plastic domes and timber huts, modern would be a metalloy bio-habitat. Modern could mean an electric ground car in a culture of horse-drawn transport. Here on Lerdun it ought to mean some at least of the scientific developments of the galactic civilisation.

On worlds where the tentacles of the many economic organisations held the power those worlds would be developed in the ways best suited to the econorgs' devious purposes. On an open world, and there were a surprising number of them, the state of civilisation could vary widely and wildly. Cantacle came up over the horizon and Hook slid the flier low. They would have been picked up on probe radar screens already. If he acted suspiciously, he might be shot out of the air without question, as the company goons had shot up the telephone booth.

Hook put the flier down.

He felt too vulnerable in that shining blue plastic and metalloy hull. He slid the canopy open and jumped to the ground. The metalled road lay a mere five hundred metres away, and cars passed in a steady trickle of headlights. The stars poured down their brilliance. Hook had no idea if Lerdun possessed a moon or a collection of satellites. He helped Pera down and started off for the road.

They stumbled across a stubble field in the darkness and Pera swore as she tripped in an irrigation ditch. Hook helped her up and then kept his left arm around her waist. She felt lithe and bouncy, very nice, and he was aware of the feel of her flesh beneath his fingers, moving against her backbone. They walked to the road and halted, out of range of the flaring headlights.

Hook waited until the road towards Cantacle was clear of cars. A vehicle approached travelling towards the city, not going too fast. He took deliberate aim and shot the rear nearside wheel off.

The car slewed, screeched, braked, finished up broadside on across the road.

Hook ran across.

A man was just climbing out, shaking his head and yelling, all at the same time, like a manic mummber.

Hook hit him over the head, let him fall to the ground, stuck the Tonota into the car and told the alien girl with the blue hair and cerise eyes: "Get out, lady, and you won't get hurt."

She, like a fool, started to scream.

Hook lifted her out and held her.

Pera said: "Oh, no – you wouldn't!"

"Not this time, maybe," said Hook. "But if I had to, I would." Now why in hell was he chattering away like this? Just get on with what had to be done. He put the knuckle of his fore finger under the alien girl's ear and she collapsed quietly.

She wore an emerald-green glitter-gown, cut low, and she had a nice figure. Hook didn't know what planet she called home. He could understand the human man taking her for a ride to the city, though.

He dragged them safely to the side of the road and left them. He stood back, and then returned. He pulled the man and alien girl side by side and then arranged their arms and legs. He thought that the guy ought to thank him when they woke up.

Back at the road he took the car by the fender and dragged it across the road.

Within moments the next electric car screeched up, sounding its horn like a drunken banshee. The wrecked car blocked off the highway. The newcomer stopped. He got out and started to walk up to the wreck, flexing massive shoulders, his head sunk down between them.

He was a Krifman.

Tough, Krifmans were. Fancied themselves as the bully-boys of the galaxy. This representative wore lounging robes of some dark colour; but Hook knew he'd have plate-clothing underneath, and a damned great gun holstered at his belt and a little Delling or other horror up his sleeve. Hook walked up and the Krifman swung about. Hook hit him in the guts with the right knee and brought the Tonota down butt first on that harsh rounded skull.

The Krifman dropped.

Just to make sure Hook hit him alongside the ear.

The car was empty.

"Get in, Pera."

As though all this was a fresh nightmare, Pera went to the Krifman's car and got in. She flopped back in the sprung seat with a sigh. She was tired. And no wonder.

Hook deftly winkled through the Krifman's clothes.

Wallet, with enough money-metal to make life a little different from here on in. The gun, as he expected, strapped to the bulky waist. Hook slid the gun out and left the holster. There was no time to disengage the nasty little Gel-Mix up the alien's sleeve.

The wrecked car was pushed to the side of the road. Hook gave it a final shove and it toppled off the metalling.

Back in the new car he started the electric motor, touched Pera's knee, flicked the car into high forward and said: "Get some sleep."

Pera Sotherton surprised Hook then.

In a firm voice, she said: "All right, Mister Hook. If we're in this together, and have to do these terrible things – just how much money did you get?"

Hook chuckled. "One thousand in bills, and some loose money-metal."

Pera, like anyone else, didn't bother to ask after the Krifman's wrist credit-card. Ordinary credit-cards were sometimes used. Most folk had their credit-card neurally sealed to their left wrist. That way it was a part of you. It couldn't be removed without removing the hand and wrist. Hook would have done that, without a second thought; but the severance destroyed the card's validity.

"Get some sleep."

"All right. But wake me up when we reach Cantacle. I'll have to ogle the goons to get us in, won't I?"

"Maybe. Not if we barrell through."

"That means you do expect the enforcers to be waiting for us." Pera yawned, and stretched, and said in a voice more slurred from fatigue than Hook cared to hear: "You'll never drive right through. They'll crisp you."

"So let me think. Go to sleep, you –"

"Sure. Plug-ugly Hook, I'll go to sleep."

They'd be in Cantacle in less than an hour, even at the sedate speed Hook drove the car. They checked into a traffic pattern and Hook kept strictly to every rule in the book. Other cars flashed past in the exit lane. Pera closed her eyes and slept. Hook sat relaxed, not feeling tired yet, a little hungry, as he had said; but perfectly capable of going on for a lot longer yet before he needed sleep.

Cantacle came up in a flaring mass of coloured lights, a raucous wide-open city of garish pleasures and follies, a place where tired men could recuperate and smart girls make a fortune. Hook drove the car carefully along the road which widened and turned into a light-hung boulevard. Traffic thickened. There seemed to be, as far as he could tell, no signs of a traffic hold up. No road blocks, then. Maybe the central computer here on Lerdun wasn't so all-fired hot.

The small screen mounted centrally over the fascia came alive. A tape-recorded voice said: "Welcome to Cantacle. We hope you enjoy your visit. You are now requested to switch your controls to auto-traffic. We will take good care of both you and your vehicle."

If Hook didn't tumble the switch that would put the total guidance and speed of the car under the control of the traffic computer at city-centre, a traffic-cop – of whatever breed they employed on Lerdun – would drop out of the sky onto the roof of the car and the whole shebang would be lifted up to be dumped in the city pound.

Traffic-cops for many thousands of years had been renowned on all the civilised planets for their trigger-quick temperaments. They were a fact of life. You had to live with them, wherever you went in the civilised portions of the galaxy.

Taking the routine traffic instructions as a good omen, Hook tumbled the switch and the tape-recorded voice said: "Thank you. Where do you wish to go in Cantacle?"

"Plaza Hotel."

"A moment, please." Sundry clicks and buzzes, then: "I am sorry, sir, there is no Plaza Hotel in Cantacle. May we suggest the Mars-Venus?"

So they'd body-tagged him for a terrestrial, then. Blast it. If they routinely checked on all entrants to the city they'd check out his sweat and hair-follicles and whatever with those found at the store robbery and match them. Hook said: "That will be fine."

"Thank you, sir. We hope you enjoy your stay."

The screen died and the smiling face vanished. Computers. He looked across at Pera. Then he nudged her in the side with an elbow. He had taken his hands off the wheel, for the car now whisked along boulevards and streets with a sure certainty, passing other traffic, diving into tunnels, soaring out along flyovers, all controlled from traffic-centre.

"Hey, Pera. We're here."

"Get off!" she said.

Hook nudged again.

"Cantacle. Mars-Venus. I just hope they have hot and cold running robots, that's all."

The car slid beneath a portico and the door hissed open.

CHAPTER SIX

IN the galaxy of the hundred and first century you were a member of a multi-system conglomerate, a unit of a union, a world-government employee – sometimes a member of an armed service – in which happy event your econorg, union, government or service stood in loco parentis and would look out for you and protect you.

The loner, the person outside the system, was not protected.

Ryder Hook was a loner. He had no credit card. But he did have a bankroll now, a stolen roll of money-metal, and so could pay his way for as long as the cash held out. Until that happened the service he would receive on Lerdun would exactly match what he could pay. When the roll was exhausted –

"The hell with that!" said Ryder Hook, and took Pera Sotherton's arm and marched across the foyer to the desk robot. He punched out his requirements.

Pera said: "Oh!"

"One room, Pera."

"I suppose so."

The robot clicked and lights twinkled and a recorded voice said: "You are most welcome to Mars-Venus. We have all the Terrestrial solar-system outworld luxuries you may care to sample here. Earthpeople a specialty. Room number nine five three. Your luggage will be handled. Thank you."

The elevator was just that, a real elevator with an electric winch and cables and a car. The Mars-Venus believed, evidently, in creating an atmosphere. An olde worlde atmosphere. An anti-grav chute would have been an anachronism here.

Inside the room, which was tastefully furnished in the late Martian Dynamic style of circa two thousand years ago, Hook threw himself onto the suspended bed. "They'll find us, I estimate, before too long. Until then, Pera, you sleep." He dialled out for a light meat meal with a salad and a bottle of white wine – he wasn't choosy which solar system it came from.

Pera ate with a ladylike delicacy that admirably concealed her hunger. Hook tore up the meat and wolfed it down. Pera slept. Hook lay down, got up, prowled, lay down again. He wished he had a sensing kit, then he'd know when the goons were approaching. As it was, his estimate of the Lerdun central computer was low, and he had figured out their chances to a nicety – or so he hoped.

He looked at Pera, asleep on the bed, with a scrap of flame-red briefs showing through her torn trousers. He had no interest in her, save as a means of getting off-planet. But he found he had no real desire to take chances with her life.

Along toward dawn of the twenty-eight terrestrial-hour cycle of Lerdun he roused her. He dialled out for breakfast and they gulped down orange-juice, bacon and eggs – it was all real food grown on-planet and not synthetics – and four cups of tea each. Hook disliked coffee, as any civilised man did.

He eyed Pera.

"Something glamorous, I think," he said. "But businesslike."

Pera made a face and put down her tea cup. "I wear clothes like that every day, Hook."

"Sure. That's why you wear 'em today." He pointed at the dial-monitor. "Order out the kind of suit that would take you into business meeting, and make the directors' eyes pop at the same time."

"All right. But I can't see why –"

"Do it!"

Pera ordered an aquarius metal skirt, very demure until she crossed her legs and revealed just how far it was slit, and an aquarius metal bolero over a lemon blouse. This meant her breast cups had to be lemon too, and she chose half cups with a nipple opening. With a few accessories of coral and ivory, she looked ready to take a secretary's place and destroy the concentration of her boss. Hook chuckled. He had been chuckling a lot, just lately, and he wondered why.

"You'll do. Not too much makeup. Remember, you are

the efficient secretary, and the sex is an unfortunate by-product."

"Thank you!" sniffed Pera.

They had to pay for the night's lodging. Credit card worthiness would have relieved them of the humiliating business of reading the bill and paying in cold hard cash. Many people on the modern worlds never handled – scarcely ever saw – money from birth to death.

They stepped out and a robot voice said: "You wish your car, sir?"

"No." Hook didn't have to think about that one. He took Pera's elbow and they walked out into the morning sunshine of Cantacle.

Pera's new shoes made a silly click-clack on the sidewalk.

That had been a mistake.

Hook's own black boots were soundless.

As in most departments of Hook's life he would face a problem squarely, look at it straight on and then askew, calculate it out, figure the angles and the odds, and having done all that would barrell right through, as he had planned, if necessary, to have done last night gaining entrance to Cantacle. Having said all that, though, it would have to be added that flexibility gave Hook the capacity to change plans with ftl rapidity. That silly click-clock of Pera's shoes could be tolerated for what he wanted her to do. Afterwards, she'd have to run of her own free will on bare feet, bloody or not, if she wished to stay with him.

The day looked promising, with weather forecasting sunshine and a few late morning showers, just to freshen things up a little. Hook walked with a swing, taking stock of everything, aware that he must meet the next emergency before it had time to develop too far.

In Cantacle business was transacted as in any other city, and people were going about their day's work. Banks were opening, shops were issuing taped invitations to enter for marvellous bargains, some sideshows were already on the road warming up the cast for the sterner work tonight. In a little park flowers bloomed under the sprinklers and robot gardeners chuntered to and fro clipping and sweeping.

"How much did your ticket to Albeira cost Pattens, Pera?"

"I've no idea. Mr. Porten arranged it – he has a travel secretary to care for details like that."

Hook marvelled. Pera must be a bigger wheel than he'd imagined.

"Guess."

She made a face, walking along in the sunshine. "Ten thousand?"

"About. Anyway, we don't have the kind of money-metal to buy transportation off-planet. Even low style, frozen, costs more than we have left from that Krifman's wallet."

Hook chuckled again. The Krifman's money had bought a night in a hotel and meals, a new outfit for a girl, and left a little for sightseeing. Just about what the human man had planned for his little alien girl with the blue hair and cerise eyes, and the balance still wouldn't buy them passage off-planet.

"So we can't use money-metal to buy a passage –" Pera stopped talking. She stopped walking. She turned to face Hook. Her eyes snapped at him and he realised she'd finally caught on.

Then she said something that shook him; for he hadn't realised, as he should have, that she'd thought his scheme through and disregarded it and hadn't bothered to tell him because she figured he'd have sense enough to see it wouldn't work.

Until now.

"If you think I can call out to Pattens, to Mr. Porten, and ask them to space me money-metal – why, Hook, you're a cretin as well as a chancroid."

He had to say it.

"Why not?"

She waved her arms about under his nose, dangerously.

He caught her elbow and hustled her along the sidewalk. It was too early in the morning for way-out activity and he didn't want to attract that kind of attention. Later on the weirdos would rise and stagger out and then anything would go on the streets of Cantacle.

"Why not?" she spluttered. "Why, you big ape! Pattens don't have an agency here. No-one is going to handle their affairs without so big a cut it wouldn't be worth it."

"You mean your Porten wouldn't pay to have you back?"

Hook looked down his nose. "He must share the same opinion of you I have."

She tried to kick him, and he slapped her rear and they walked on for a space in a huffy silence.

Hook fumed. If all he had been dragging this girl along for was not to pan out, he'd been wasting his time. Hook had wasted too much time in this man's galaxy to relish that.

At last he spoke to Pera in a voice that made her stiffen and glance at him with those large blue eyes, and then look away, hurriedly. Hook knew his face was not a pretty sight.

"You're going to call this Porten character. You're going to tell him you're stuck down here on Lerdun and you need cash for transportation. Two tickets. If you play any tricks and just get one passage – well, Pera Sotherton, it won't be me who stays down here with these gonils."

"I believe that, Hook! You'd do anything to save your own skin, and devil take anyone else!"

"Of course."

"Chancroid."

"We'll go to computer house. Save time. And get a smile on that beautiful puss of yours."

"You!" Pera was shaking with a rage she recognised to be useless and that only made her all the more angry. "You think I'll do anything you say!"

"Yes."

"I won't!"

"If you don't smile and look sweet when we get into computer house I'll tan your backside for you, right out there in the foyer."

"You wouldn't dare!"

"Don't be childish."

Pera marched on. This man, this chancroid, this plug-ugly devil Hook gave her a freezing and yet scorching pain right up her spine. She knew he'd hit her. He would smack her bottom soundly, right there and then, if she didn't do as he said. What kind of a man was he, anyway? Was he a man at all? Maybe he was an android, a clever fabrication of steel and plastic powered by isotope engines and muscled by spring-steel, with a nuclear recirculator for a heart and a computer for a brain. He could be.

He damned well could be.

54

He hadn't shown the slightest sexual interest in her, not even when she'd changed into the new dress. And she knew with a certain complacency that her face and figure had excited enough men – important men! – in the past.

Maybe this famous Ryder Hook was merely a walking metal man.

They stepped onto a strip and were whisked along. Cantacle hummed right along all around them. Computer house turned out to be an imposing fifty-storey block with overhead passenger ways curving through thin air from neighbouring buildings and with no flier park atop the roof – up there the authorities had sited an anti-aircraft battery that would lock-on and blast out of the sky any approaching flier that did not respond in the proper way to the sequence of identification calls.

The entrance had been carved from a single crystal of ancara, and the faceted stone gleamed and glittered like an underwater fairyland in full colour in the subaqueous lighting. Hook marched Pera straight up to the first vacant booth in the long row to the right of the entrance. The place was not too busy as yet, and a human attendant was idly dusting a robot attendant under the strip lighting. The rows of booths were mostly empty. Hook pushed in, plonked Pera down on the seat, and started in on summoning up the magic science of the deeply-buried computer complex under the building.

When he had the master on line, he leaned back and said to Pera: "Now get through to your boss and tell him. Two tickets, mind."

"I'll try."

"Tell him there might be a deal for him here. I assume you'll speak in code?"

"Naturally." Pera's scorn gave her a valuable outlet for her seething emotions. What nut was going to talk openly through some system's computer and communications centre when all the galaxy had open ears?

Signals sped through cables and were flung in space-time fracturing swarms between the stars. An adaption of any of the various drives that powered the metal hulls of spaceships at ftl could hurl simple binary signals with an acceptable time lag.

Pera punched out the call sign that would take an image of her

55

face and the sounds of her voice across the light years to Albeira.

You didn't have to know how these things worked to be able to use them. How many people knew how to pilot a starship? Come to that, in the old days, how many people knew how to fly an aeroplane or drive a train and yet used them as a mere matter of course? How many people could repair an electric speak writer?

Pera said: "It is very important. Please tell Mister Porten that Miss Sotherton must speak with him."

Hook grunted. He perfectly understood this mister and miss business; it indicated to the underling to whom Pera was speaking that she and Porten were past the taynor and tayniss stage in their relationship. That would be valuable.

After a procession of flunkeys' faces came on the screen and were passed, the screen writhed as though going through an imperfectly adjusted scrambler. Hook was watching the charge meter ticking over. The money-metal was being spent at a great rate and he kept feeding it into the avaricious slot that kept demanding more. If Pera didn't get through to Porten before he ran out of cash – then Hook surmised grimly that some other poor devil in Cantacle would have to be deprived of his wallet.

It was, considering the circumstances, exceedingly difficult for Hook to feel sorry for anyone who got in his way; but feel sorry for them, at this moment of waiting, he did. He was a soft-hearted slob, really, when you came down to it.

"Pera?"

Hook looked at the screen over Pera's shoulder.

"Mr. Porten! Thank the Great Salvor! I'm in terrible trouble, Mr. Porten –" Hook thought she would burst into tears.

"There, there, Pera. It's all right now. I wondered what had happened to you."

Mr. Porten was not a human being.

To be strictly accurate – and Hook had a passion for accuracy, which for a man with his bizarre lifestyle was a vice he could ill afford – Mr. Porten hailed from Kircher. This meant he looked like a somewhat loosely constructed wickerwork basket with hairs sprouting everywhere and the interstices filled with gleamingly brilliant jewelery. Somewhere under the hair and among the faceted gems he had four arms and two legs and a sensory nerve centre and system. He perceived by means of a multitude of tiny eyes situated on various of his hair endings, as he had sound locators and heat sensors and all the usual five senses of Homo sapiens. It was not true to say he was not human; humanity is not the sole prerogative of Homo sapiens. He was a human being; he was, in the basic meaning of the word, a man; he just simply wasn't a Terran.

Pera began babbling a whole string of words that Hook hoped would not alert the constantly-monitoring robots and cause them to switch on their recorders. Later analysis would inevitably break any word-of-mouth code like this unless it was a personal code arranged between the parties on the basis of information only they could possess.

He nudged Pera, one eye on the meter.

"Hurry it up, Pera. The cash is just about shot."

"I do hope your third, fifth and seventh wives do you honour, Mr. Porten, and your joy with your second and fourth wives is complete."

"Indubitably, my charming Miss Sotherton, and I trust your next liaison will give you exquisite pleasure."

The screen died and Hook exclaimed: "There's one more to go! And I put the damn thing in!"

Pera laughed.

"I don't like paying for something I don't get," said Ryder Hook.

"Don't fret over a one. The tickets are being arranged. Mr. Porten can put them through Interstell-Imp, and he's letting us have enough money-metal so we can travel in style."

Hook remembered the little furry Cailiang woman from the doomed *Iquique.* She'd been Interstell-Imp. The sound of money tinkling with that extravagant musical chiming of money-metal cheered him up. Maybe they'd get off Lerdun without the need for more killing and destruction. Hook tried always for the quiet life. The trouble was – the trouble always was trouble.

The habits of a lifetime could not be easily broken and so Hook paused before leaving and let his eyes seek out what dangers there might lie before him on the street, as he looked back to see if anything smelled wrong in the foyer. Everything looked clear. Taking Pera's arm he went out into the sunshine.

As they walked along towards Interstell-Imp's agency in Cantacle, Hook relished that sunshine. That wasn't old Sol shining down up there; but a galactic adventurer quickly grew accustomed to the feel of many different suns.

The robot dispenser had everything ready for them in a plastic wallet. Pera reached for it and Hook's brown hand closed over her own slender fingers. He squeezed and she gasped and dropped the wallet. He picked it up and flicked it open. Two tickets, singles, in style, Lerdun to Albeira. And five thousand in money-metal. Well, Porten wasn't mean, but he wasn't a spendthrift, either.

"Let's get to the spaceport, Hook."

No answer was needed. Hook dialled for a cab and they swiftly whisked over the rooftops and along the invisible aerial lanes towards Cantacle's nearest spaceport. This lay only a few kilometres outside the city limits and was one reason for Hook's choice of Cantacle over some other cities whose spaceports were shared among a complex of conurbations.

"The goons haven't picked us up yet, and here comes the spaceport. I figured they might have fed that item into the computer; but they can't have."

"You hope."

"You still think Pattens had trouble making a deal with Interstell-Imp, don't you? If they did, we'll soon find out."

They might appear to the casual eye merely two people walking along the sunshine-filled streets of Cantacle, taking a cab, laughing and relaxing. The truth that they were a hunted pair, sought for crimes against the state, made through that darkness the colours and the light and the brightness that much more brilliant.

Vainly wishing for something that was not possible had been a pastime Hook had never indulged in. But, just at the moment, he rather wished his Jack Kinch circuits could cut him into the local planetary police network. Ironic, here he could ease his way into the private communications and control networks of any number of econorgs and system governments, scattered over a vast area of the galaxy; and he couldn't listen in to what the petty local police chief was telling his men and robots to do about the pair of fugitives. Irony was a bitter word at times.

The cab decanted them at the entrance and a pedway took them smoothly into spaceport reception.

The murals displayed a tasteful representation of the *Amphite and Leon*, a verse-drama attributed to Proctor Beavis who was reputed to have lived circa eight thousand or so, Earth reckoning, although some authorities credited the Riffian, Haffler, a shadowy minor poet of half a dozen centuries later. Whoever it may have been, Hook glanced at the murals and approved.

He could not fail to miss the brief wink of light as a spy lens cunningly mounted as a part of the mural swivelled in its everlasting monitoring of the reception area. Hook moved smoothly away with Pera and headed for the rest room complex. He halted at a drug-store counter where all the goods under their display perspex would pop out for the right credit card presentation or money-metal. He collected various items he would need.

"Why don't we board, Hook? Albeira is scheduled on flight fifty, and that's due out in an hour."

"We'll catch flight fifty, Pera. Now shut the orifice and twinkle the feet." He led her to a rest area booth and closed the door on manual.

He looked at her critically, taking the brown wig out of its plastic wrap. "They'll have information on us, and pretty good descriptions; but they won't know we have money and tickets. So if we can fool them into thinking we're two other people –"

"If only we were!"

"– they've no reason to query our tickets. So I'll turn you into a different girl." He took out the cosmetics. "Any girl different is going to be an improvement."

"You're a burst ulcer, Hook!"

"Shut up, or you'll get facial gel in your mouth."

Working with the quick practised touch of the professional Hook built up the chin and jaw lines, thickened the nose, coarsened the cheeks. The spray-gel solidified instantly into a supple skin-like coating. He lined the forehead and trimmed the wighair-line into invisibility. The blue eyes he left. Blue eyes were normal enough and he hadn't bought a retinal colour kit.

By the time he had finished tinting and shading he had added thirty years to Pera Sotherton's face. She scowled at him in a most ferocious manner.

"Now take off your breast cups, and –"

"What?"

"Take off your breast cups. Tie this scarf around you and flatten out. You're a dumpy old lady, now, so remember to keep that metallic skirt slit closed, and the bolero fastened. The clothes make you look like an econorg's lower echelon executives' secretary, aping styles of her juniors. The real business miss who runs the show. Got it?"

"I've said you're a chancroid, Hook, and a burst ulcer, and a candidate for advanced pustular syphiloderma, and I'll go on telling you you're a Pasteurella pestis –"

"Sure," said Ryder Hook. He reached out a hand and unlatched the lemon blouse. "Take off your breast cups – or I'll do it for you."

A devil got into Pera Sotherton, then. The rest area booth with its shower and toilet facilities, its hot-air blowers and its array of dispensing equipment might be a sterile environment for severely practical purposes. Hygiene had swept away many of the current swear-words. But the devil reared in Pera and wouldn't go away.

She faced Hook.

"Right, Hook. Do it."

Pera fancied that would take the wind out this plug-ugly, and she prepared to be cutting with him.

Hook flicked the metallic bolera down over her shoulders, opened the lemon blouse. He unhitched her left breast cup and threw it on the soft-plastic-tiled floor. He took off the right breast cup and hit the left with it. He put a hand holding the scarf around her back, under the blouse, put the other hand around the other way, pulled the scarf through. He held both ends of the scarf, one in each hand. He pulled. Pera surged towards him. Her face was so congested with fury she almost spat at him. Almost. She stared at Hook's face and she shivered and lost all interest in the devil rearing in her.

"I'll tie this damn tightly, Pera. Would you care to do it yourself?"

She wouldn't give him the satisfaction of a sob as she grabbed the ends of the scarf and knotted them up, pushing her flaunting firm breasts down and flat.

"There, you bastard! Is that what you want?"

Hook nodded. He began to work on his face. Pera did herself up and watched – and gasped.

For before her eyes Hook as she had known him vanished. The facial gel sprayed cunningly here and there altered the planes of his face, smoothed out the arrogant lines of power, softened the jut of chin and the beak of nose, pouched the eyes. He combed the brown hair the other way and pulled it back, spraying facial gel down to heighten the hairline. He checked both of them, Pera by tilting her head this way and that, roughly, and himself in the mirror over the basin.

"Right. You're Dorothea Brooking. I'm Alan Hardacre. No names on the tickets, as I said. We go through. I'm your boss. If they want to see my credit card I have a story to cover that." Hook did not add that he did not intend to blow that cover story until he had to.

They went out of the rest room area and headed for embarkation.

"Walk like a little old lady, you cretin!"

"Slob!"

She shortened her stride and tried to keep the athletic swing of her hips into a shorter, more matronly humping. Hook shuffled along, sniffing and peering and mumbling.

At the gate leading to the transporter that would take them out to flight fifty a robot checked tickets and credit cards. At its side, his hand resting on his Tonota Eighty, stood a golden coveralled Customs man. He eyed the passengers with the look of a man bored with life and aching for knocking-off time.

"Just let's get off this godforsaken planet!" said Pera.

"Just a few more minutes and we'll be on the transporter and way out to the starship. Now act like an old dear, for Dirty Berti Bashti's sake!"

The couple in front flashed their wrist credit cards and showed their tickets. The man, small and warty-looking, said something to the Customs man. The guard pushed up from his slouch and said something back and the woman with the runt

61

lifted her hand and shouted vilely at the guard. Hook heard what she said. "You're a disgrace to Lerdun, that's what you are! Great slouchy slommicky oaf!"

The couple walked on towards the transporter and the guard put both hands on his black belt and glared after them. Hook shoved the tickets into the robot's slot. It gurgled and chunked them back with a section missing. He picked up the tickets and the robot said: "Boarding fee, sir. Please show your credit card."

"I'll pay in cash," said Hook in his mumbly voice.

The guard swung around. He looked mean.

"Where's your credit card, sir?"

"I'm paying by cash."

Pera said: "Interstell-Imp will vouch for my card, taynor."

The guard took out the Tonota Eighty. His lips ricked up. He was a beefy, well-fed man, with shining lips, and he couldn't stop the look of satisfaction on his face.

"So you're not with an econorg, bud?"

"Not at the moment. I'll just pay the boarding fee and then we'll get along –"

"Not so fast. So you're a loner, bud?"

"Yes."

"Well, now. I needed something like this to freshen up my duty." He surveyed Hook. "So no one is gonna come alooking for you, gonil. You're not protected."

"I can pay."

"Sure, curd. Sure, you can pay. You can pay me. Hand over your bankroll."

"What –" whispered Pera.

Hook did not hesitate. He handed over the bankroll. "Now can we board?"

"Board? Pay the robot the boarding fee, then you can board, gonil."

"You are a government man of Lerdun," said Hook. "You have just taken all my money-metal. So what do I pay the robot with?"

"That's your problem, gonil. Clear the entranceway, there! There's folks waiting to board."

Half a dozen inhabitants of Lerdun were waiting. They were smiling to see this loner get frisked by a government man.

"Please –" said Pera. "It's not fair!"

"Nothing's fair if you don't have a credit card to protect you," said a woman in the crowd. She laughed. "Let us through."

Pera stood there, stunned.

Hook debated – uncharacteristically.

It had all happened so quietly, without fuss, without drama, but smoothly and lethally and with fatal precision. No great dramatic blood-spattered moments had been necessary. They were as effectively trapped down here on Lerdun as they had been before contacting Porten of Pattens.

"Let me through!" shouted Pera. All her resources had broken down. She screamed and dashed for the transporter. The guard stuck out a foot. Pera tripped, went flying, sprawled along the concrete. Everyone laughed. Hook did not laugh.

Pera staggered up, dishevelled, frantic, distraught. Her wig slipped.

A voice cracked over the hub-bub: "What's going on here? Clear a way, there!"

The Customs man grabbed Pera and hauled her to her feet. He pushed her at Hook. He was enjoying this.

"Get out of it. Take this drab with you. If I catch you trying to board illegally again I'll run you in."

He knew, as they all did, that the threat meant nothing beside what he had already done.

That harsh authoritative voice cracked again. "Hold still! You there! C'mere."

Instinctively adhering to his disguise, Hook hunched around, his face indicative of extreme fear, a facial contortion masking the hate that struggled to blaze out. He looked and he regretted his disguise had given him no opportunity to hide the gun he had taken.

Contemptuously, Goton Telander pushed his way through the crowd, his black uniform dominating and menacing, his face showing the first signs of the triumph that was his.

CHAPTER SEVEN

Hook had grown tired of Lerdun.

They wouldn't let him depart peacefully, all the ills he had brought them had been of their own doing. He was a man who believed in a justice that meted out justice higher than mere planetary laws, was Ryder Hook. They wouldn't let him go. Very well, then. He would have to do what, he supposd with a sigh, he should have done at the very beginning of this tedious affair. He would simply bash in a few skulls and take what this planet owed him and then space out. For a quiet man with a love of peace, Ryder Hook was often forced to be violent and vicious and exceedingly nasty.

He hit the Customs man in the guts. He took the Tonota into his own hands and swung the muzzle at the jeering crowd.

They screeched with fear, and ran, and threw themselves to the ground, and screamed some more.

As he had in the Customs House yard, Goton Telander, when gunplay began, made himself scarce. He vanished into a side corridor and his parting shot splashed Delling-gel-dis over the staggering guard. The guard melted. He flowed and dissolved into a disgusting mess, a slimy puddle on the ground.

"Oh, Hook! We can get into the starship now!"

Hook grabbed her arm.

"Act your age, Pera! If we board now they'll know where we are, have us trapped. We've got to get to hell out of here and start all over again."

"Oh, no!"

"Oh, yes! Come on!"

Hook had not fired the gun. He held it big and bulky in his fist as they ran back through reception. People got out of his way. Outside, Hook knew, he'd have scant seconds in which to make good their getaway. He bundled Pera down the steps, stuck the gun into the belly of a puffy Tenebrian – a man with the features of a wizened monkey and the temperament of a mouse – and told him to precede them to the car he had just quitted. Off to the rear the crash and roar of a panic-stricken crowd added force to his words.

"Get in, gonil."

"But – but –" stammered the Tenebrian.

"In!" Hook slammed the alien into the car, said to Pera: "Take off one of those damned stupid shoes of yours and if this curd squeaks, hit him." He started the car and roared it away from the reception area. People jumped wildly out of the way. Hook was feeling in a vengeful, an unpleasant, a downright upset mood. Blasted womb-regurgitant Lerdun government!

"Where are we going, Hook?"

With a choking whine from its overdriven electric motor the car howled along the boulevard. Hook hunched over the controls. A police car cut in from the side and tried to swing broadside on in front so as to force them to stop. Hook sent the car full-tilt at the police car. His nose struck the side, a screeching sound of ripping metal and a shower of sparks were followed immediately by a grating rending as the police car skidded along the pavement. Hook rammed up full acceleration and forced the car on. As he flashed past the police car he saw a Lerdun policeman jumping out brandishing a gun. Hook burned the car and the policeman with a single blast from the Tonota, aiming with snap-shooting precision through the window. Breeze blew in through the vapourised glass.

"Oh, Hook!"

"Keep your head down."

He wheeled the car around the first corner.

He barely made it.

The opposite building abruptly puffed a gout of flame and smoke from its store front. Masonry collapsed. The shot from the entrance had only just missed them. The turn-off from the boulevard had taken them away from the road to the city. In no time at all they had left the last buildings and were thrumming along between orchards and truck-farms. The countryside looked green and fresh and parsecs removed from dead guards and burning cars.

Hook looked up through the perspex roof window.

A flier circled up there.

"Goddamn Lerdun bastards!" said Hook. He hauled the car up in a wide skidding turn and plunged bodily in among a pear orchard. The trees were widely-enough spaced to allow the car through and the branches concealed them from visual observation. He just hoped the infra-red detector gear in the flier was not good enough to pick them up with his own bafflement gear operating. He jumped out and hauled the Tenebrian after him.

A frightened whiskery face gazed up at him, the eyes round and filled with tears.

"You've caused a lot of trouble, gonil," said Hook. "I only hope you're sorry for what you've done."

"Yes, taynor, yes, sir, I am – I am!"

"Don't forget it."

Hook grabbed Pera by the arm again – that arm would have permanent finger marks ground into it soon – and hared off. If he could reach the road on the other side of the orchard there would be transport along soon. He hoped the flier would stop to investigate the car.

Pera panted along after him. For Hook this shambles on Lerdun was becoming an affront. He had not been acting as Hook would normally have done. Not at all. He wondered if this was because he had the Sotherton female along. No – maybe he was going soft. He hated to kill anyone; but if he had to he had to and if it was a choice between being killed and killing, Hook had no need for second thoughts.

That slob of a Tenebrian, now. What harm had he done? Nothing – apart from being a part of a galactic civilisation that refused to allow Ryder Hook a normal life. By the token on his wrist, that man was merely one of the billions who had outlawed Ryder Hook.

The farther road was a mere dusty track, used for servicing the pear orchards. The flier appeared over the trees, hummed down. Hook lifted the Tonota and blew the perspex nose of the craft into splintered flames.

The flier gyrated crazily. But it did not crash and made some kind of landing along the road. Hook didn't wait to see. With Pera being dragged along he bolted for the opposite orchard.

The tree before him frizzled. The trunk blackened, the leaves crisped. The tree burst into flames.

Hook dropped flat. He hauled Pera down.

He swung the Tonota and cut down three men who were running for him, their guns still firing and heating the air into a cauldron.

A fourth man flung himself flat.

Well, there was only one answer to that. If a man took cover you simply burned the cover right out from under or over him. The men shooting at him were using Marker Burners, guns without the disintegrating power of the Tonotas. They were slower acting, too. Hook aimed at a clump of dirt behind which the man had gone to ground and fired. The gun clicked empty.

"Goddamm it to hell!" snarled Ryder Hook.

The man stood up.

He held the gun pointing at them. The trees at Hook's back burned with a harsh crackling, and scented smoke drifted.

"You offworlder bastard!" shouted the man. "You burned Sammy!"

Shouting back threats now would be futile. The man did not fire. He wore a russet-coloured tunic and yellow pants. He was not a planetary enforcer, then. He still did not shoot, yet he must be able to see Hook and Pera quite clearly now.

So – he didn't shoot.

Maybe he wanted to torture them a little.

Let him try . . . Ryder Hook stood up and lifted his hands.

"I ought to burn you both, right now!" The man's eyes were glazed and his lips worked, with a thread of spittle dribbling down. Hook wondered if they had been aliens if the man would have been able to control himself. "Walk, you gonils! And if you make me shoot I'll burn your feet off, so help me!"

Another flier slanted down. Like the first, now that Hook had a chance to examine the craft properly, it was not a police job. They got in. Men and aliens crowded them. The flier took off with that swooping whoosh and rush so typical of the sports craft and whistled across the sky, headed back for Cantacle.

The man who had captured them took out a pack of stim-gum, stripped off the sticks and handed them to his companions. They were all chewing away as the flier slanted in for a landing atop one of the planetary econorg agency buildings.

The rooftop was heavily guarded by anti-aircraft weapons.

There were two landing parks up here, one, the larger, clearly the day-to-day general service park for clients. The flashing spark-sign proclaimed for all to read the name of the multi-system conglomerate whose agency building on Lerdun this was.

Interstell-Imp.

From the street-level counter they had so recently picked up the tickets to Albeira and the five thousand.

The other park was smaller and private and here they touched down. They were shoved out and down an anti-grav shaft. The guns in the fists of the men were displayed openly, without any reluctance. Hook was perfectly aware of the score here, and he guessed Pera would know it, also. After all, she did work for Pattens, and one econorg was as bad as another.

"My offer still stands if you want to run."

"I need both my feet," said Hook.

Below roof level they were plunged into a different world.

Outside lay the city of Cantacle, functional, glittering, filled with people about their daily work, waiting for the evening when the fun and games could begin. Inside the agency building of Interstell-Imp they might have stepped into an Arabian Nights extravaganza for tv. They left the anti-grav shaft and walked through jewelled grottoes where scented air wafted, past elaborately equipped restaurants, through rest areas and gymnasia, beneath swimming pools englobed in stasis fields that held a thousand tons of water suspended between marble walls. The sheer exuberance of luxury would leave a first timer flabbergasted with the superabundance of wealth. Colours, lights, scintillatiae, precious stones and furs and feathers and skins, all the outpourings of a hundred thousand worlds in space had been carefully sifted to bring together the most precious items into this jewelled wonderland.

Pera sniffed.

"A tatty joint compared with Pattens."

"Still and all." said Hook. "Hedonism, luxury, barbarity of design. It all adds up. Interstell-Imp look after their people."

"Luxury I'll grant you. It's plush, all right – and vulgar."

Hook really shouldn't be concerning himself over the mental wellbeing of this girl, whoever she might be, who had tagged along with him and, having served her purpose, could be discarded. But he felt some relief that these surroundings, so luxurious to the unwonted eye, had brought back her spirit with their familiarity. Econorgs provided rich playgrounds for their people off duty. Pera must, in a weird way, feel at home.

The galaxy was inhabited by many races and although it would be true to say in the widest sense that nature's evolutionary ideas tended towards the typical in construction, the variety was broad enough to satisfy the eclectic. Most races in the galaxy had one head, with various forms of sensing organs thereon. Most had two legs and two arms, arranged tastefully about the trunk. A lot had tails. Some had forms of body covering that could not be called skin. There were permutations of many delightful kinds on the basic morphology. Around them now passed many weird beings. To cater for their needs the playground and recreation areas of the agency building had been planned to incorporate alien ideas of beauty and function and pleasure.

The whole place twinkled and glowed and hummed with energy.

A woman wearing a white apron stopped them in a small room that glowed a mellow green, shading deep emerald at the wainscot level to a pale leaf green at the cornice. She looked hard and competent, with hair severely cut into a helmet shape of black lacquer. The men who had brought Hook and Pera here halted.

"Take the man up to suite eight nine able, Stokes. The girl goes with me."

"But –" said Pera.

A gun jabbed Hook in the small of the back. Mad he might be, hasty when it came to punching noses at the right time, Hook knew when the time was right only to have his backbone blown out through his stomach cavity.

Pera went off, the woman holding her arm with a slick professional grip. Hook felt she ought to find the finger-ridges in that slender arm.

"Up, curd." The gun waved, unanswerably at the moment.

"*Hook!*" screamed Pera, dragging and falling, her wig all askew. Her blue eyes pleaded.

"They're not the Lerdun police, Pera. We'll find out what it's all about —"

Stokes, the man with the russet tunic and yellow trousers, tapped Hook alongside the ear with the gun. "Move, you gonil! One more chance and I'll sever your feet. *Move!*"

Obediently, for that was all he could do just at the moment, Hook moved. Pera was dragged off, screaming. Hook had seen and heard many girls dragged off screaming before. Pera worried him, though, even though he owed her nothing.

The company enforcers took Hook to a suspended cell in a larger room deep in the guts of the building. Unlimited wealth could buy almost unlimited facilities, and Interstell-Imp had not stinted on equipping this agency. The cell walls were invisible, consisting of englobed lines of force more unbreakable than metalloy. The whole cell hung suspended in an anti-gravity well, apparently hanging in mid air within the larger cell. In one corner stood a lavatory shower toilet complex coupled to a disposall. A divan bed completed the furnishings. Hook was stripped naked and thrown up through the aperture, which he could not see, and which was closed after him by the flick of a switch.

Philosophically, he lay down on the divan and went to sleep.

No doubt, given the time and the incentive, he could have broken out of this kind of cell; he was not vouchsafed the time and he did not have the incentive. He was far more interested in finding out just what Interstell-Imp wanted with him.

When he woke up an amplified voice from a speaker mounted above the toilet complex said: "You will wash thoroughly, all over, and disinfect yourself. You will remove that stupid disguise and then dress in your own clothes."

Hook did as he was bid. He knew that his clothes had been minutely searched. They were clean. Although he sometimes utilised the electronic marvels of this galaxy, Hook was a man equipped to deal with problems with the resources embedded in his skull. He pulled on the drab tunic and trousers and black boots philosophically. He guessed, too, that his whole anatomy had been subjected to electronic search. Well, they'd find nothing of metal or plastic in his head, and the organic implants had been blended to the brain tissue. If they wanted to know if he had anything in his head, they'd have to trephine.

"Jump!" commanded the voice.

Hook jumped down out of the aperture and was met by the weapon of Stokes centred on his anatomy. Stokes had discarded his Marker Burner and held instead a Wharton model ninety three. This fired a sheaf of micro-needles and could paralyse or kill – most painfully – and was used as a common-sense weapon inside a building where a Marker or a Tonota would blow the place apart.

Stokes took him through a devious maze of passageways. Hook could have dealt with Stokes at any time and taken the gun and started hunting up the exit. He had an idea Stokes wanted him to try. Hook was more interested in finding out what was going on, and the best way of doing that lay in talking to the person who wished to talk to him. They entered an ante-chamber where an armoured robot checked them. It took Stokes' gun away and lapped metalloy cords around Hook's arms and throat and hobbled him with a twenty centimetre loop, so that he had to totter forward like a fun-girl on her last mission before retirement.

Stokes picked up a nasty little plastic truncheon.

"This is loaded with paralysis-gum, Hook. You get funny and I'll lay into you, got it?"

Hook didn't bother to reply or react, and they went through the crimson gem-studded folding doors.

CHAPTER EIGHT

JEDGAR Kaston sat in his metalloy force-field cocoon and considered the data coming up on the screen before him. Jedgar Kaston as the planetary manager of Interstell-Imp on this open world of Lerdun had a mind for greater things. He had chosen to have his planetary headquarters built here in Cantacle as a kind of defiant act against the blue-nosed government authorities. Jedgar Kaston was a man who oozed power, who controlled many other beings, who had a mind seized with the desire for ever greater power, a man whose ambitions would never be slaked short of the complete overlordship of a multi-system conglomerate.

Even then, even then, Kaston would admit to himself, he would want to go on.

Jedgar Kaston was not a member of Homo sapiens.

He had begun life as a perfectly normal mal, of Homo mal, a race old in the galaxy, and had early showed exceptional gifts, rapidly rising within the hierarchy of Interstell-Imp, the econ-org into which, through family connections, he had been born.

He had chosen as many beings did to become a dynaman. His legs had been amputated – quite voluntarily and at considerable cost – and replaced by a smoothly functioning anti-grav system. His arms had been amputated and replaced by a pair of heavy duty grabs and a pair of delicate tentacles. With the latter a dynaman could experience all the tactile sensations of a normal being, as many a lissom girl in Jedgar Kaston's office could testify. He sat within a metalloy cocoon, his torso comfortably padded, self-powered, self-contained, a machine directed by a living being. Very few dynamen ever complained they had been shortchanged on the deal.

He liked to employ mals about the place. With their chunky

bodies and heads with the faces so grim and forbidding, with the high cheekbones and slanting eyes, the bristly hair and the tube-like ears, they reminded him of home. He doubted if he would ever now bother to revisit the Jertling system, home of the mals, where he had been born, unless profitable business could lure him there.

He had absorbed the information supplied to him from a number of sources, some legitimate, most not so, and compared the total with what Interstell-Imp's head office had to say about this man Ryder Hook. The fellow was a pest, that was clear. Just what RCI had been up to, Kaston was not yet sure. This curd Hook would help him to find out.

Interstell-Imp had less reason to love RCI than almost any other multi-system conglomerate. All econorgs felt themselves menaced by all other econorgs, of course; but alliances were possible. Pattens had done him a good turn.

The cardinal rule for any member of an econorg was simple, direct, and extremely brutal in its observance.

An econorg employee was totally loyal to his multi-system conglomerate, above any loyalties to race, solar system or religion. It mattered not what shape you were, not what god you worshipped, not what planet you called home. All that mattered was your complete and absolute devotion to your econorg.

Jedgar Kaston within his shining cocoon, hovering smoothly in comfortable reach of his desk and its many electronic out and inputs, waited quietly as Stokes brought Hook in. Hook hobbled forward. Kaston as was habitual with him, summed up the being before him instantly, in terms he would understand. Hook was dangerous. He was tough. He was a menace to any well-run econorg. Once he had sucked him dry – and used him on the GCC business if he proved suitable – there would have to be an end for Ryder Hook.

"Do you know who I am, Taynor Hook?"

Hook took in the office. the desk, the dynaman behind it, and the implications of that polite use of taynor, and relaxed into an easy stance within the hobble that masked his readiness to leap instantly at the shining cocoon and get his hands around the neck of the dynaman. He looked like a mal, and they were bad news to any human being.

"No."

"You would do well to address me as sir."

Hook didn't reply. Stokes lifted the plastic club; but Kaston waved him down with a tentacle and flicked the controls on the readout. The screen cleared. Kaston began to read out.

"Ryder Hook. Born on Earth, a so-called Homo sapiens, on Leaf day, six thousand and eighty five –"

"That's your alien reckoning," said Hook. "I was born by old Earth reckoning on the first of January, One hundred nought one."

"Ten thousand and one." Kaston had by now accumulated so much power with Interstell-Imp he often marvelled at his own tolerance, and wondered if it was really a case of a Werkler cat and a Werkler mouse. "A pity you Terrans haven't made better use of your time in the galaxy."

Hook simply looked at him, storing away impressions. The man was in the prime of life. He had chosen to become a dynaman for the savage power the metal arms gave him, the speed and untiring energy of the antigrav. The man was dangerous, then.

"I have a dossier here on you Hook. You are known to my conglomerate. You were an employee of Rocket Consortium Interstellar. You volunteered for the RCI Powerman Project. I understand that was designed to fit puny human beings like you for work on heavy gravity planets."

"That's right." Hook could remember how he'd been inducted into the project. He'd not been getting on in RCI as he felt he should. He was as smart as the next guy, quick and alert; but his friends got the plum jobs and he was left slaving away in the electronics office along with youngsters. "I'm surprised you know about that, though. It was supposed to be secret."

Kaston chuckled. "Secrets have a price-tag like everything else. Your father was an electronics designer with the spaceship yards. Your mother was, before her marriage, an actress." Kaston nodded to the screen across which the information flowed. "It says here she was a promising young actress."

"So I've heard."

"You have a brother and a sister, both younger than you.

74

Your father was killed in a spaceship yard accident about which there is little information —"

"Not surprising." Hook remembered the long agonising days he had spent asking questions and being met by polite blank refusals. *Something* had happened to his father in the yards. No one was talking. But — his father was dead. "They hushed it up."

"I see that you were fired from the Powerman Project." Kaston looked up sharply, his dark eyes hooded on Hook. He looked like a lamplit Buddha in a golden alcove, squatting there in his womb-surrogate. "Why?"

Hook didn't shrug. But the affected gesture would have fitted the question. "I've no idea. They worked on me — I assume you know the details of what they were doing — and then they said deleterious side-effects were showing up and they threw me out."

"You were a failure."

"RCI evidently thought so."

"You enlisted with Earth's armed services. It was more difficult to obtain information — I understand you went through a full course of training and saw action in that Bendola flare-up."

"Yes."

Hook's attention was now centred totally on this mal. He knew a great deal. Hook just wondered how much he knew of what Earth's armed forces had done to him — did this dynaman know Jack Kinch?

Jedgar Kaston had now reached the end of the basic information he possessed on Ryder Hook; but he was a man to whom bluff and intrigue were a necessity of business dealings. So, smoothly, he went on: "After that you became a nuisance. You were in trouble with various conglomerates. You belonged to none and so have no wrist credit card — no credit card of any sort — and as a loner you hated those who had spurned you."

"I don't hate anyone," lied Ryder Hook.

"You came to this planet seeking trouble."

"We were spacewrecked. The bastards of the Lerdun government treated us —"

"Treated you exactly as the law prescribes. I have made it my business to investigate anything untoward on Lerdun, Taynor Hook. Your landing of the life shell impressed me. You were stupidly naive afterwards, however –"

"Have you ever been a covenanted labour-unit – a slave?"

Stokes lifted his truncheon at this and again Kaston waved him down. Stokes bridled.

"Whyn't you let me bash some respect for you into him, Manager Kaston, sir?"

Hook stored that away.

"Taynor Hook has great respect for me already, Stokes, and for the power I wield. He knows I can crisp him where he stands."

Hook had observed the variety of orifices below the lip of the transparent hood of the cocoon and without bothering to figure out which were what and what kind of weapons were housed there had worked out a system for dodging them if he had to wrap his fingers around this Manager Kaston's throat.

"You see that I am a dynaman. Let us take you back to the RCI Powerman Project. I can take it this was a kind of dynaman objective: one that you, perhaps, did not wish to finalise?"

"Sure," said Hook, lying again. "Who'd want to walk around without arms and legs."

Watching Kaston, Hook conceded the dynaman a point. The planetary manager gave no single sign of reaction to the taunt. He merely leaned forward and with his left tentacle flicked a couple of switches on his orange/brown console. On the wall at right-angles to the curtained windows the picture that had been silently running all this time slowly dissipated. Hook had taken in the pictured scene. A massive volcano, harsh and upthrust against the sky, tumescent with unreleased power, kept vomiting chunks of flame and lava, and subsiding, and rumbling forth once more. Clearly, the volcano was about to explode.

Now the screen within the ornate picture frame writhed and cleared to reveal a dancing girl of the Shashmeer, all long white legs and impossible breasts and hips, and tinkling ankle bells that rang a carillon chime as Kaston increased the gain. The dancing girl contorted her body lasciviously. Hook liked his women built the way they were styled on Earth. He looked back at Kaston.

"You pity me, Ryder Hook?"

"I pity no one."

Conversationally, Kaston said: "The force screen two metres before this desk not only stops a projectile or a human body, Hook. It destructs them. I offer you this information."

Hook did not reply. He had found that saying nothing often paid greater dividends than mere words, hot from the unthinking thalamus.

Kaston turned up the music. Alien stringed instruments twanged a lascivious accompaniment to the dancing girl's twining limbs and bouncing breasts. A panel in the far wall slid aside and a Shashmeeri girl undulated in, twin to the pictured dancing girl gyrating on the screen.

"Dance, Shirie," commanded Jedgar Kaston, smiling.

The girl danced. Hook felt only a mild interest, for overblown women had never interested him. This Shirie could dance; there was no question of that. She pouted her rich soft lips at the dynaman and ogled Hook as she flaunted past. Then at a finger-tentacle-click from Kaston she sidled closer to the planetary manager. She passed through a pair of red arrows on the floor. Hook marked those red arrows, and as Shirie undulated around Kaston, nuzzling his face, flaunting herself before him, Kaston noted Hook's eyes and said: "I lowered the screen. You would fry if you tried to pass."

Now Shirie was working with quick passion on Kaston, her tongue busy, her lush body pressed close to his torso within the shielding cocoon. Kaston flicked open the front panel. Stokes standing at Hook's side wiped his forehead and then ran a finger around the collar of his russet tunic.

Kaston's tentacles caressed the girl, ran over her body in lascivious movements that brought moans of pleasure from her — whether faked or genuine Hook neither knew nor cared. He saw what Kaston was up to, and had he not wished to bash the creature over the head and get to hell out of here, he might have admired the dynaman for his insolence.

"Well, Ryder Hook. Do you still pity me?"

Hook kept down his flash of anger. Anger was all too easy and treacherous.

"I've told you, Kaston. I pity no one."

"I really think you should call me sir. Stokes! Take him to

the discipline cell. And, Hook, listen. I have a proposition to put to you in which you can in aiding me aid yourself. When you return you will be in a more – malleable – frame of mind."

"Out, you!" said Stokes, and flicked Hook lightly with the truncheon. Some of the paralysis-gum stung his left arm and the limb hung, useless. "Out, curd."

Hook looked back at Kaston. The dynaman had unhitched Shirie's gilt breast cups and his tentacles were clearly sending him all the sensations a normal mal's six fingers would have done. Shirie was lifted by one of Kaston's power-arms and bent and giggled before him and as the doors folded close Hook saw that on that score, at least, Jedgar Kaston needed no pity.

Ryder Hook knew about discipline cells.

Stokes took him out to the armoured robot who unlashed the metalloy thongs and Hook rubbed his legs with his right hand. Returning blood circulation tingled and throbbed and he made no effort to conceal his pain. His left arm might just as well not have belonged to him. Stokes laughed.

"You think that hurts, gonil? You wait 'til the discipline cell tastes you! Haw!

Hook waited until they reached the discipline cell doorway.

The entrance had been fabricated from skulls. That was a fancy Hook could ignore; symbols have power only when they are understood, and then only if the understanding is allowed to work and ferment in a fearful brain. Inside, the cell lay ruby-red under the lights, stark, bare, waiting, alive.

Hook kicked Stokes on the ankle.

The return blow from the truncheon revealed fast reflexes, and Stokes hit Hook across the back of the head before he had time to halt his reaction.

Hook pitched to that ruby-stained floor, unconscious.

Ochram Koltner pursed his lips and tut-tutted.

Koltner was a mal, like Kaston, his employer. He had the high slanted cheekbones, and eyes wide-set and upward-angled like wizard's eyes, the bristly hair and tubular ears, and his chunky body was clad in a one-piece metal-fab suit all in ruby red. From the black belt around his thick waist swung a multitude of crude instruments – crude not in construction for many were marvels of engineering; but crude in purpose.

"You're a right clunky, Stokes. How can the cell discipline this curd if he's out like a drunken coliman in a sporting house? Do you think Manager Kaston is going to promote you for work like this?"

Stokes' mouth was suddenly dry.

"He jumped me! You saw it. I had to hit him –"

"He wanted you to hit him." Ochram Koltner rolled one of his tubular ears between his fingers, a gesture characteristic of mals. "A clever one. It'll do him no good, though. He is to be returned to the Manager Kaston after he has been disciplined. I can wait." He stirred the prostrate form of Hook with a plastic shoe, and then kicked. He grunted. That helped.

After Koltner had waited three hours or so Hook awoke to find himself sitting, alone and naked, in the centre of the ruby-red floor. He ached. But he could feel his arms and legs, and feel, too, the grinding headache that came as a gratuitous aftermath of the paralysis-gum. Hook cursed. He'd been too clever, or Stokes had been too stupid. He had aimed at having the enforcer paralyse his other arm, or a leg, let him be subjected to the discipline-cell with some slight advantage.

But the idiot womb-fugitive had knocked him out.

And now here he was, naked as the day he was born back on Earth, cringing under the expected onslaught.

Without warning, the torture began.

CHAPTER NINE

THE voice of young Ryder Hook's academy instructor floated in his head. "Science, of course, is only a tool to be used by intelligence; but a tool may turn in a man's hand."

"Or a tentacle, sir!" chirruped young Tearik, waving his own six tentacles annoyedly in the warm air of the classroom.

"RCI, to whom we all look for salvation, has been good to you, Tearik minor," said the academy instructor, reprovingly. "We are as well aware as you that tools may slip in the grip of even six tentacles."

At which the class guffawed at young Tearik's discomfiture.

Ryder Hook floated peacefully on an azure cloud. Below him lay the future, and above him the past, and on either hand the unknown galaxy.

Why did he not prosper as his classmates prospered in RCI? Why was he always stuck with the routine humdrum jobs? Young Tearik, now, had gone as planetary resources adviser halfway across the home spiral arm. "You will volunteer for the RCI Powerman Project, Ryder Hook!" and months of pain and toil as the medical scientists of RCI subtly altered his body cells, and his bones and musculature took on some of the attributes of living metal. "You will volunteer for special training, Sergeant Jack Kinch!" and months of surgery as the cunning organic grafts were implanted in his brain, undetectable by the best electronic probes. Earth's armed services required his total loyalty, as a civilian econorg would so demand of their enforcers and employees. A mission to spy for Earth should be a great and holy crusade; where, then, the glory in it all?

Ryder Hook screamed.

He wasn't on Earth, he wasn't involved in the Bendola flare-up. His mind was a leaping, hunted organism cavorting through past scenes and events of his life. Jack Kinch? A notorious assassin, sir, and should be hanged! Jack Kinch? A dangerous man, sir – if he is a man – and should be shot!

Ryder Hook screamed.

Many planetary managers trembled at the name of Jack Kinch. Many heads of multi-system governments shook when they heard that Jack Kinch might be making a landfall on any of their planets. Jack Kinch? Jack Kinch was never Ryder Hook – how could he be? Ryder Hook was a failure, a man hunted by the Boosted Men, a man marked for destruction. Ryder Hook was a galactic adventure; Jack Kinch was a notorious galactic assassin.

"No!" Ryder Hook screamed as the onslaught of pain mounted and his own brain turned in on himself and tortured him with remorse and despair and final dissolution.

Just before that stage of foetal withdrawal, the discipline-cell situated in the bowels of Interstell-Imp's Lerdun agency relented, and eased up, and the palpitating circuits died, and Ryder Hook could open his streaming eyes and swim upwards to the light and to sanity.

"Enjoy yourself, curd?"

Ochram Koltner chuckled and rolled his ear tube between his fingers.

"If I didn't enjoy myself, you bastard, you did!"

"Certainly," Koltner chuckled. "Certainly."

The ruby-red floor dimmed into maroon and then into darkness. Stokes pussy-footed in and hoisted Hook out. Hook felt as though all his bones had been broken and his blood congealed into a black pudding. He shambled after the enforcer, with the minder of the discipline-cell trotting after, having himself a good time and sorry that this Earthman had been taken out of his six-fingered hands.

What Hook had suffered in that cell only he could know, for everything which had twisted and tortured him had sprung through the perverted use of science directly from his memory into his agonised immediate participation. One silly mistake as a boy, a painful accident, a severe chastisement – all these acrid memories normally lay buried and containable. That damned discipline-cell flooded the immediate mind with total awareness of them as of the here and now – total remorse, total recall of pain and agony. No wonder Ochram Koltner often dragged screaming wrecks from his cell, their minds shattered past the point of acceptance, driven insane.

"This curd, Hook, now," said Koltner reflectively to Stokes. "He looks tough. I'd have liked to have had him in there a little longer. My discipline would have broken him."

"Your discipline, Koltner?" Stokes had got over his fright about knocking this Hook senseless. Manager Kaston had been busy in the interim and the delay had not mattered; but Stokes wanted to get back at the discipline mal. "Not yours, Koltner – it's the cell that does it, the cell that's alive."

"True," agreed Koltner. His pride in the discipline-cell was such that Stokes couldn't annoy him. "One thing – I'm glad I don't know what it was this clunky suffered in there."

"Me, too," said Stokes, and kicked Hook to move faster.

Because he had suffered a punishment-period in a discipline-cell before this, Hook had the theoretical remedies at his finger tips; problem was to make the theories work. He drew deep breaths and flexed his muscles and he made himself look squarely at some of the things he had gone through – again – in there, and by doing that drive them back into the abysses of his mind.

Along the corridor he began to feel something like the Ryder Hook he knew ought to feel. Koltner stopped on the corner and said to Stokes: "He's all yours, now, Stokes. If Manager Kaston decides to send him back to me –"

He didn't finish the sentence.

Hook's naked toe took him in the groin. Before his shocked scream could ring out Hook swivelled and hit Stokes in the guts. He had judged both blows nicely. Both Stokes and Koltner doubled up; but they did not collapse, they were still capable of receiving further blows. Hook delivered those blows. He was aware as he struck and struck again and the blood spouted and the bones broke and grated, that he should not enjoy doing this. Hatred – yes, he was no wishy-washy saint – he knew what a good honest grudge was like. Enjoyment in inflicting pain? No. No, he detested pain whether being administered to him or being dished out by him. Pain in the modern galaxy was an obscene thing. He took no relish in doing this. He did it because he did not believe any old man or any old mal should be able to knock Ryder Hook about without understanding the folly of that action.

Just before Ochram Koltner lapsed into unconsciousness, Hook bent beside his bloody and broken body and whispered into one tubular ear: "I'm not frightened of your disciplinary-cell any more, you goddam-stinking bastard. It's done all it can to me."

And, to Stokes, he whispered, clearing the blood clotting the man's ear: "Next time, Stokes, I might kill you and put you out of your misery."

He walked away down the corridor. He didn't bother to take Stokes' gun. That last remark – it was no threat. Hook had long ago come to the conclusion that to threaten anyone was usually counter-productive. Best get on with it. But that last threat had been a kind of jam on the bread.

He walked slowly up to the armoured robot. The thing came alert and a red light flickered frantically. It extended its tentacles holding the metalloy cords. Hook took them in his hands, and then, so swiftly that the cords became threads of spun light, he threw and looped them around the robot's tentacles. He brought his clenched fist down on the red light. The robot squealed and tried to say: "You will be disciplined for this –" And then it went: "Disciplined – urrgh, urrgh, squeal . . ." For Hook had ripped away its control panel and dived his hands inside and ripped out a contorted maze of intestinal wiring. He threw the mess on the floor. Just how much money-metal had he just fouled-up? He didn't know. He didn't care.

He went through the crimson gem-studded folding doors.

A tri-di of Jedgar Kaston in his silvery force-field cocoon crouched behind the desk. The room, apart from Hook, was empty of life.

"Most impressive, Taynor Hook. I am glad you did not kill Koltner. He is a mal. As for Stokes – a term as a covenanted labour-unit may spruce him to higher aspirations."

"Do I talk to this thing?" said Hook, gesturing to the tri-di representation. "Or are you afraid to be seen yourself?"

"Taunts bounce off me, Taynor Hook. I still observe you do not address me as sir."

"You mentioned a proposition."

Down in his apartments in the heart of the agency building Kaston let a smile flicker across his face and the expression was faithfully recorded on the tri-di simulacrum sitting behind his office desk. His apartments were so vulgarly and ostentatiously decorated as sometimes to make him wonder if he should not clip his ears and become a monk. A half-naked Earth-girl finished peeling a grape between rosy fingers and popped it into Kaston's rat-trap of a mouth. Kaston liked this Beulah routine. He had learned it from a Terran passing through. The Terran – he was not Homo sapiens – had liked it, also, and Kaston had caught the habit.

"Proposition?" he said. "You are in no position to make a deal of any kind save an immediate walk to my prison cells."

"You'd have to drag me."

"I think we would."

Hook realised he was expected to take that remark either way. Again he had to score a point for the dynaman.

Jedgar Kaston considered. He felt ninety-nine percent confidence in his assessment of this wild Earthman. If what he would be sent to do could be done, Ryder Hook could do it.

He spelled it out simply.

"I am having a little tiresome difficulty with GCC at the moment. I see my way clear to wiping them out and taking over their credit, their customers and their outlets on this planet."

"Sure," said Hook. He sat in a single-legged chair that accepted his weight and shape and adjusted itself accordingly to give him the most comfortable support. "It's going on all the time. Econorg eat econorg."

"Just so. You will penetrate GCC and obtain details of certain of their planetary operations. Armed with that information I can move in. You will, it goes without saying, be well rewarded."

"With a Tonota blast up my back?"

"You have my word as a mal."

Hook knew the virtues of discretion. The word of a mal was

84

as worthwhile as an aeroplane in space. But he had formed an opinion of just how far he could go with this creep.

"If you are caught, Hook, as you may well be, there will be nothing to connect you with Interstell-Imp. Nothing. If I send one of my own mals – well, you see the folly of that, I am sure. And if I farm the contract out, I am at the mercy of the unscrupulous assassin who takes it."

"You said photograph information."

"So I did, so I did, to be sure. If Nellinger happens to be in a suitable position, I would, of course, expect you to – ah – dispose of him for me. That should be obvious."

Well. Hook killed his smile. This was one for Jack Kinch.

"Obvious. Still, it's nice to know you did tell me."

"I do not think you can afford to refuse, Hook. I should then have to dispose of you. You have tasted my discipline-cell. I have other means, also, to ensure painful death."

"I don't doubt it. It fits."

Riding Hook's crude sarcasm, Kaston outlined the means to be taken to disguise Hook, to issue him with a credit card that was as near a perfect forgery as made no mind, and to insinuate him into the GCC econorg agency which was situated in Pearlhampton, the capital of Lerdun.

"One last thing, Mr. Hook –"

"Taynor," said Hook, without really thinking.

At last, and for the first time, Hook felt he had got under this dynaman's force field skins.

"One thing, Taynor Hook. Whilst you are carrying out this task for me I should remind you that Tayniss Pera Sotherton enjoys my hospitality. Should you fail me I shall treat her with especial care." Kaston flicked a tentacle. Sherie glided from a lounger in his apartments and appeared as another tri-di simulacrum beside the dynaman. Kaston began to fondle her. "I am sure I need be no further explicit."

If Hook replied with what was, after all, the truth, and said: "You can do what you damn well please with the Sotherton bird," he would gain nothing. And it might drive Kaston into dealing with Pera when there would be no need for him to treat her with anything other than his mask of courtesy. So Hook kept his space ration hole securely battened down.

"Good. You are a businessman, Taynor Hook."

"God forbid the day!"

"Maybe that is why you are a failure in the galaxy."

CHAPTER TEN

ELECTRONICS engineer, grade four, Abel Klark – galactic failure, although currently a pseudo-employee of GCC – rode the downtown pedway in Pearlhampton and reflected that he would have liked to have had Shaeel along with him now. The Hermaphrodite had been on a number of highly illegal and stimulating excursions with him before, and ve always claimed to enjoy them. But then, Shaeel was as unpredictable as any member of ves race, and as infuriating into the bargain.

Ve was a good scout, though, and Hook – whose brand new identity as proclaimed from the near-perfect credit card strapped to his wrist was Abel Klark – felt an unaccountable loss. He couldn't believe that he, the supreme loner of the galaxy, could be pining for ves company. Not even Shaeel, good scout though ve was. No. It was simply that Ryder Hook appreciated expert help in nefarious expeditions.

Hook strode on, passing other people and aliens standing on the pedway and allowing themselves to be carried along. The sun that was not old Sol blazed down. The air smelled sweet and clean. Plenty of traffic chortled along the boulevards, the electric motors near-silent and completely free of pollutants. The buildings reared everywhere, with their interconnecting flyovers and pedways. Below ground the tunnel complexes demanded by any large modern city were functioning smoothly. The whole show delighted Hook.

Kaston had equipped him with a clumsy ear-speaker and throat-mike – a non-surgical inside-the-throat job – and Hook was in constant touch with Interstell-Imp's apparat control in Cantacle. A mal girl called Elva was on control at the moment. She sounded as tough and efficient as any mal; but Hook had been giving her the benefit of some caustic remarks.

"You great gonil, Hook! Don't draw attention to yourself!"

She could see where he was going by means of the clumsy lapel button spy-eye they'd given him, affixed to his uniform tunic. Compared to the sophisticated equipment – all organic – that he carried from the implantations made by Earth's armed services – Hook seldom cared to remember them as EAS – the electronics supplied by Kaston were mere clockwork. But they would suffice if he was not challenged and examined. That would be up to him.

"I'm supposed to be happy and carefree, Elva."

Her voice sounded in his ear from where she spoke to him, half-way across the planet back in Cantacle. He had a buddy of Stokes', one Churferen, as back-up man here in Pearlhampton equipped with a flier and a small laboratory. Churferen must stay in the background.

"You'll be so carefree you'll blow it all."

"Worried, Elva? Tell Kaston his investment isn't in danger yet."

He stopped at a corner store, suspended on antigrav stilts halfway between two major road arteries, with double access, to buy a packet of stim-gum. Hook did not use it himself; but it paid to have a pack handy.

Elva's worried voice crackled in his eardrum.

"Don't you dare use your credit card, Hook! It isn't backed by an account. The goons will have you inside metalloy bars in no time at all! Watch yourself!"

He paid for the stim-gum with money-metal and received an old-fashioned look from the girl managing the store's dispensing robots.

"Cheer up, chicken," he said to her, going out. "I've three wives to support on my credit-card and I don't want another."

The store girl gaped after him and Elva's voice blasted into his ear. "Cretin! Imbecile! Terran curd!"

"And if I said mallian murk, you'd be upset, Elva. There, I can tell by the quality of your silence."

At last she said: "Get on with the job, Hook. Manager Kaston is being linked into the net once you're inside."

"Then you'd better not step out of line, had you?"

"Bloody Earthman," she said, her voice vinegar.

88

Hook chuckled. He was on a job which he understood, he had no serious worries for Pera Sotherton, he most certainly did not intend to be caught, and, in short, life was once more hurtling along more interesting grooves.

What made the irony more enjoyable was that Kaston and Interstell-Imp imagined he was a cowed man working for them in ever-present fear that some awful fate would overtake the girl with whom he was passionately in love. They imagined he was quaking with concern for Pera Sotherton, and ready to dance to their tune. What a gang of Charlies!

The truth was they had given him this credit-card, pseudo though it might be and not susceptible to an intense scrutiny; but perfectly adequate to get him through the perils of the day. In addition they had given him an excellent disguise. It was a better job than the one he had done so hurriedly in the rest area booth in the spacefield reception back at Cantacle. He had black hair, trimmed in the fashionable artisan's cut, yellowish cast to his features, and they were long and thin and mournful, and he wore a smart pair of lime-green coveralls with GCC's emerald green and pilcher red insignia blazoned over the lapel, concealing the spy-eye button. Oh, yes, Interstell-Imp had done him proud.

He could have boarded a spaceship in this get-up. He tended to doubt if the credit card would really fool a starship payment robot. They were notoriously thorough.

He carried his electronic tools kit on a long strap over his left shoulder. Kaston had vetoed the idea of carrying a sleeve gun – a Delling or a Parkat, say – but had felt a large and elderly and overly-ornate Zag would suit a middle-low grade electronics engineer. Hook had agreed. A Zag of whatever model fired a projectile that, in modern terms, was truly huge, something like two point five millimetres. The ostentatious butt and side-plate decorations, all writhing dragons and eagles and monsters of the deep, fitted an electronics man who fancied his luck and couldn't afford a powergun.

You didn't have to carry a gun these days, of course. If you wished to do so, you might. Hook would always remember his father saying to him "Well, lad, if you carry a gun when you grow up, make sure you know how to use it, keep it clean, and if you have to use it – which I trust you never will – then make damn sure you hit the other guy first. *See?*"

Hook had seen. Sage advice.

Temptation to Hook was like some venomous reptile from an alien planet, to be watched and studied and steered-clear of, something not to be treated too lightly, and yet also something not to be afraid of. Gambling, like smoking and stim-gum, he could resist as though they were hemlock. He would drink now and again; but having seen an old Earth Armed Services pal, Ginger Lewis, crawling along with no legs below the knees and with his guts trailing along the alien ground after him – shot to blue-bloody-blazes when blind drunk – Hook had no time for drunks. You couldn't be one hundred and one percent efficient – as their special services instructor phrased it – when you were blotto.

Mind you, with the quirky metabolism he had, Hook could drink most beings under the table, roar and shout and gamble all night long, smoking like a chimney, chewing stim-gum until his hair frizzled, with a wench on each knee, and get out in the morning and clean up the local situation.

That was just Ryder Hook; he took no pride in that.

When he saw the central municipal museum across the pedway Hook didn't change stride; he simply altered his approach. He knew he couldn't stop himself. He went up the escalator into the building and felt the familiar air-conditioned mustiness close around him, and he sighed.

"What now, Hook?" Elva's voice crackled against his ear drum. The speaker might only be the size of a pinhead; it produced an almighty volume.

"Just taking a look around."

"Well, get out of it! Manager Kaston expects you to be inside the GCC building by noon. He's coming on net then."

"Interesting," said Hook. He aimed the spy-eye in his lapel at the skeleton the size of two fliers on end, towering in boney starkness against the far wall. "Look at that! A dino, with three brains, and six legs, and two tails. Wowee! You sure don't find 'em like that back on Old Earth."

"Now cut this out, Hook! What are you, a museum nut?"

"Yes," said Ryder Hook.

That was the temptation he could seldom ever resist.

"You stupid Terran curd! If Manager Kaston comes on net —"

"He will, Elva, he will. Look. Over in that case," Hook bent closer, shoving the electronics gear out of the way. "A creature who might have been the original inhabitant of Lerdun — only that was before it was called that, before anyone knew it existed, orbiting that sun up there. He might have developed into some kind of human being, if —"

"I live here, Hook. This is my planet."

"Sure, Elva. It says here he couldn't adapt to an ice age they had back a million years ago. Sad."

"I'll make you sad — you had a heterodyne whine in your ear-hole lately?"

"You do that, Elva, and by Dirty Berti Bashti's breeches I'll hoick the speaker out of my ear — and the rest of this gear monitoring me, too, you hear?"

She fumed. But she knew Hook would do as he said.

Hook spent a pleasant three hours in the museum. Just letting his mind wander free in these places, without seeking any particular objective, delighting in all he saw, gave him the keenest pleasure. He had plenty of vices, he knew that. He wouldn't take a blow lightly. He would bear a grudge if he didn't attempt seriously to rationalise out whatever insult he had been offered. His vices were legion; but none could give him the unalloyed pleasure prowling around museums could always afford.

Precisely at noon he was back in the entrance foyer.

Jedgar Kaston came on net. Elva spoke mighty small when giving her report. Kaston's tones dripped like ice into Hook's ear.

"Taynor Hook. May I remind you you are working for me now and I expect results? Think of Ts Sotherton. I have much to do —"

"Sure you have," said Hook. He let the spy-eye pick up the gaunt bones of the dinosaur again. "Look at him, Kaston. He had plenty to do, too, one time. Just think. Another couple of hundred years and you'll look like that."

Kaston did not reply.

91

Chuckling Hook sauntered out into the noontime sunshine and ambled along towards the GCC agency building.

Hook smoothed that Devil's hoofprint out of his forehead as he wandered into the side entrance of the GCC building.

Acres of synthi-marble flooring, mellow under hidden lighting, railway-lines of counters, humming with transactions and deals involving a thousand planets, efficient robots, pretty girls in the short-skirt and cape fashions currently in vogue with GCC personnel, alert guards, blank-faced enforcers, checking everything and everyone – all the busy scene reminded Hook of the mindless activities of pent-animals in cages. He had deliberately turned his back on all this and had thereby become an outcast, a pariah, a loner of the galaxy.

He was not alone in this loneliness: there were other beings, human and alien, who had chosen not to belong to any econorg or solar systems government.

The lime-green coveralls and proudly-displayed badge would have taken him past the counters, along the synthi-marble floor and into the back areas where the accounting and records departments were situated. He let his velvet-trimmed coverall sleeve back to show the credit-card strapped to his wrist, and he ambled along just as any other workman summoned to a job would philosophically saunter there, chewing his stim-gum, looking for the evening and knocking off shift time, and the lurid divertissements of the capital city.

His mouth was empty although he chewed with that cow and cud rhythm the stim-gum addict doesn't even realise he has.

He offered the stripped-back pack to the girl in the short skirt and flared cape sitting at the last desk before the rear corridor.

"What a day," said Hook. He yawned, hand over mouth. "Floor thirty five. Some idiot jimmied his power outlet." He looked at the girl, at her blonde hair done up in ringlets, at the curves beneath her wax-flower blouse. "Hey, gorgeous. You doing anything tonight? There's a place I know –" He leered.

"Elevator thirty, clunkhead." She smiled at him, though, and there was regret in her voice as she added: "My date tonight is special – sorry."

"Lucky guy," said Ryder Hook, half-meaning it, and ambled

on into the corridor. Elevator thirty took him to floor thirty five in a silent whoosh as the anti-grav operated. He sauntered out, still chewing, looked up and down the empty corridor.

"No one is bothered about this area, Hook," came Kaston's voice. "I've attended a conference at GCC, before they got up my nose. You want floor sixty."

"Check. I'll ride the service elevator grav shaft. They expect me to, don't they, an electronics man, fourth grade?"

"Get on with it and stop chattering."

The service anti-grav shaft contained plain white plastic panelling and a sheer drop. Hook stepped out into thin air and whisked up. At floor sixty he stepped off, landing lightly, holding his electronics gear bag from swinging, and looked into the barrel of a Tonota Forty.

"Yes?" said the goon. He had a blue chin and blue eyes and blue lips. He wasn't a man. He had four arms that could wrap around a rib-cage and produce best bloodstock jelly. He wore lime-green coveralls, and the badge, and. Hook took comfort from them.

"Assistant secretary," he said. "Says he's blown his input. I dunno how they do it. And they're the ones who get the money."

The goon holstered his gun. "You and me both. Along there. Check at the desk before you go in. Otherwise they'll burn you down."

"So they should. That's their job, ain't it? I earn my credit card the hard way."

"You and me both."

Hook ambled off, not hurrying. He said: "If this guy Nellinger is anything like you, Kaston, he'll be armour-plated from here to kingdom come."

"Get the photo-copies of the records. If there is the chance of a hit – hit."

The equipment Interstell-Imp had installed on him – the earplug, the throat-mike and the lapel spy-eye – were, of course, GCC manufacture. Hook said: "They'll likely be monitoring their own wave bands. You can't be sure they won't cut in on this one. You'd better stop your chattering, Kaston."

"They won't break in this wavelength, Hook. Just get on with it."

Hook thought about that with some reflection as he walked down the corridor. He stayed in character to ogle a couple of passing secretaries, and they giggled and hurried on. That made him wonder if he was on the right floor. He'd expect high grade stuff up here, girls like Pera Sotherton, for instance.

The desk passed him, the sergeant there more interested in the finish of the noon race he was viewing on a smuggled tv snucked under the desk. Hook marked it all. The Assistant Secretary's office was so marked and he barged in without knocking, whistling, clattering his gear.

A sour-faced girl looked up from her computer terminal. She wore a low-cut blouse she shouldn't have bothered with, and she looked like trouble.

"Yes?" she said. "And stop that infernal noise."

"Yes, ma'am. Power outlet," Hook said, sticking to the story. "This one here?" He advanced on the second computer terminal which at that moment was silent. The girl looked taken aback.

"Tr Hoffder was using it only a few moments ago. I'm so busy – I didn't know it was on the blink."

"You carry on. I'll have it fixed in no time."

If the terminal broke into its song and dance now, spewing tape and sprinking the screen with information units, she'd want to know just what the hell he was playing at.

"Taynor Hoffder due back soon?" he asked, casually, as he flicked the off switch.

"Yes. He just stepped out for relief. Here he is now."

The door opened and a Krifman walked in.

Hook sighed.

It had to be a Krifman.

This one wore a limegreen tunic with much silver, tightly-cut pale purple trousers, and he looked too young to be the Assistant Secretary. His face carried all the harsh tones and lines of authority that carried the Krifmans so effortlessly among the stars on the backs of other people's efforts.

"Yes?" he said. "What is it?"

"Power outlet on the blink. Dead as a blown bulb."

"That's strange. I was just – have you asked for service, Ts Gertrude?"

"No, sir. You –"

94

The Krifman carried a sleeve gun. Hook would stake a whole lot more than he had going for him on that. He spoke quickly.

"It's on the blink, anyway, but it won't take long to fix."

He flicked the clasps and threw back the lid. The guts of the terminal lay exposed. They were perfectly clean and free from dust, of course, for dust was not allowed to enter here; he bent over the cavity and reaching into his gear bag produced a torch screwdriver. He lifted it as the Krifman, Hoffder, spoke. "You'd better –" Hook jumped and dropped the driver into the terminal. He saw it toppling into an interesting wedge of printed circuits.

He jumped on around. "Now look what you've made me do! The driver will short the whole shebang out!"

"I've had enough of this." The Krifman went for his gun – rather the neural and electronic circuits flung his gun into his hand. Hook dived. This was a quite normal way for a highly-placed officer to handle an intrusion of this sort. Hook went on diving, got one of the Krifman's boots into a hand and tipped him over. As Gertrude screamed and the gel-mix splashed the vase of plastic flowers, Hook hit Hoffder. He hit him just the once and then stood up and said to the girl: "Just stay still, tayniss –"

And stopped.

Tayniss Gertrude had opened her handbag and taken out a dinkly little Abdoslit and her finger whitened on the trigger.

The little muzzle centred dead on Hook's guts.

Tayniss Gertrude pulled the trigger.

CHAPTER ELVEN

THE Abdoslit might be a dinkly little lady's purse-gun; but it was designed to do just what its name suggested. That tiny muzzle orifice could shoot a curved blade that expanded prodigiously and whirled as it flew. It could shear off a man's guts, and arms and legs and head if he was foolish enough to duck. Hook flattened and rolled and the whirling blade sliced a chunk from the coverall shoulder pad and lime-green fragments scattered against the wall like buckshot.

There were two more blades in the magazine.

He leaped forward as Gertrude's finger whitened on the trigger again.

He knocked the Abdoslit up and the whirling blade cut a two-metre wide circle through the ceiling until the armour-plate of the floor above stopped it.

Hook pulled the girl roughly away as the blade collapsed and tinkled around them, a multi-ply circle of death.

He took the Abdoslit away and held it pointing at Gertrude.

"You have different items to be sliced away, Gert –"

Ts Gertrude opened her mouth and started to scream.

Kaston's voice blasted in Hook's ear.

"Kill her, Hook!"

"I don't," Hook said, reaching up to Gertrude's head, "believe that will be necessary."

He knuckled her behind the ear and the scream stopped and she collapsed. Hook let her fall to the carpet. He wasn't that much of a gentleman to ease her fall.

Six strides took him to the door. He flicked the lock to SHUT and tumbled the switch he considered the most appropriate out of the selection. ABSENT INDEFINITELY.

Just how long could an agency assistant secretary be absent without arousing the ire of the secretary?

An assistant secretary stood pretty high in the hierarchy. All along one wall banked rows of screens showed different offices in the secretarial complex, all busy, all absorbed, with lunchtime taken on the shift system. This was the kingdom the assistant secretary oversaw. Tr Hoffder ran a tidy little empire within the agency building. Hook swung the spy-eye at the still-functioning terminal.

"Start the code words, Kaston," he said. "And we'll see if this guy is high enough up to break the security."

"He ought to be," came Kaston's voice in his ear. "I paid enough to find out."

Hook over-rode the incoming chatter and shunted it into a loop. He knew the computer system here – he knew most of them but not all in the galaxy – and set up the preliminary demands. Kaston read over the code words and Hook punched them out, his powerful hands flickering over the keys faster than most top-grade secretaries.

The computer hiccoughed and a red light went on.

"Con-blast found it!" said Hook.

"Try this set, Hook." Kaston read over a fresh set of codes. This time the red light did not go on and the computer sulkily allowed that it was ready on line. Hook's badge-concealed lapel spy-eye angle was pointed onto the typehead. Hook punched out the final commands and the typehead began chuntering out groups of figures. As fast as they were produced those cypher sets would be recorded in Jedgar Kaston's office. This was industrial espionage, business chicanery, office infighting of a kind that Hook knew something about – as, indeed, would any econorg employee above certain grades – and he found the impatience rising in him. He slapped the hold and detached the spy-eye from the lime-green coverall. He balanced the thing so that it could continue to drink up the info and then set the terminal head dancing again.

He prowled.

He looked down on Hoffder and on Gertrude. He could guess at their potential relationship that had never materialised. Hook pulled Hoffder across and propped him into a comfortable position with his back against the wall. He draped Gertrude artistically across Hoffder's lap, and entwined their arms. They looked nice.

Then he prowled some more.

People who blamed the galaxy, their planet, other people, circumstances, fate, bad-luck, lack of education for the situations in which they found themselves, instead of blaming themselves, might in this situation have philosophised agonisedly about just what they were doing here. Certainly the scene held the seeds of a splendid self-analysis, filled with fraught overtones. Hook prowled with his eyes alert for the main chance.

That was armour plate up there in the ceiling. He had a doohickey in his electronics kit that should shear through; but if he did that and then climbed up through the hole he'd be met by a ring of goons attracted by the commotion and waiting for the clunkhead to emerge.

Still and all, there was profit to be made from this situation. Hook would always prefer profit to pondering.

He raked about down in the guts of the other terminal and fished out the driver. He flicked the on switch and randomly fed in a few simple commands. The terminal responded with alacrity. The computer, of course, might not have been sited in the basement beneath the GCC building. He might be on line to a planet parsecs away where GCC had developed the whole world into a single gigantic computer complex. That didn't matter. He was aware that for all his mental boasts of action, he was shilly-shallying. He glanced at the other terminal. It continued to spew information. Kaston was getting his money's worth. Hook considered.

Then he reached up and tucked his finger down inside his mouth and raked out the tiny mike. He removed the pin-head sized speaker from his ear and stowed them both safely away in a plastic envelope. Crude devices both, electronic, depending on inorganic materials for their construction.

The last thing he heard Kaston saying, as he detached the speaker, was: "It's coming in I.Q. Hook. But there is a lot more yet."

Ryder Hook tried not to be a vengeful man. When he put the computer on line with the other terminal and punched out his preliminaries, he was well aware he might alert a whole bevy of guards by not following correct procedures. He was prepared to take that chance. He worked away busily, drawing nearer and nearer to opening the computer. At last he was able to punch out the request: "Full holding details on Jedgar Kaston, Lerdun planetary manager for Interstell-Imp."

Yes, Hook tried not to be a vengeful man.

The figures marched across the page from the typehead. Hook coupled in a micro-recorder and let the little plastic machine spin the information onto a hologram no bigger than the ear speaker. He cut out the typehead. He stepped back, and was amazed to feel his thin lips stretching in a smile. Luckily he could not see his reflection in a mirror; but he knew the smile could only be described as ghoulish.

The computer disgorged all its information on Jedgar Kaston and Interstell-Imp at around the same time the other terminal announced its conclusion. Kaston had what he wanted to know about GCC. Hook had what GCC could tell him of Kaston and Interstell-Imp.

Interesting.

He supposed he would have to think about leaving. The Krifman's hand had fallen into a compromising position on Gertrude, and Hook bowed gently to them both. The pages of figures went down the disposall. Hook unlocked the door and left it on self-lock behind him.

"Sleep well, lovers," he said, and slammed the door.

The micro-record hologram went into the screw hole in the butt of the Zag and the half-length screw went back on top. Hook stepped off down the corridor, whistling.

No doubt Kaston and Elva were staring at a blank screen back in their apparat control as the spy-eye picked up the pocket lining of the lime-green coveralls. They would have stopped speaking to him, for what they said would bounce around the plastic bag in his pocket and roar back at them through the speaker. He rather liked the idea of that.

The whine would be diabolical.

The desk sergeant was reluctant to take his eyes off the finish of the two o'clock race; but he glanced up and grunted at Hook.

"Finished, huh? Now maybe someone can raise a peep outta the ass sekky's office."

"Oh, he's had to take off," said Hook, airily. "Him and his secretary, both. Power's back on, though."

But the race claimed the sergeant's attention and Hook ambled past, whistling.

An engineer with proper credentials can wander around offices quite freely. As though he was part of GCC from the day of his birth Hook went into an office, chatted up a few of the girls there – only one was a terrestrial and she was plain and dumpy – and settled behind a read-out screen. Getting the hologram out of the Zag presented no problem once his head and shoulders were inside the hood. The hologram made interesting reading. The translation from the figures made Hook wrinkle up his nose and rub his chin. On the screen marched information on Kaston that would have sent the dynaman raging with anger – and with fear. Details of Interstell-Imp's illegal trafficking in human slaves were there – GCC wouldn't do anything about that for they were similarly implicated and that was how they came to have the information. Hook had broken through many security barriers in going on line from the office of the assistant secretary. Hoffder would only be three steps from total clearance. Hook became warmly interested in the information coming up. This was dynamite. With this any other multi-system conglomerate could walk into Lerdun and topple both GCC and Interstell-Imp and take their outlets, their contacts and their customers.

But Ryder Hook was a loner.

When he had digested enough to know he held a fortune in his hands he stowed the hologram pearl back in the Zag screwhole.

If Jedgar Kaston thought that Hook would now go off and hit Nellinger, then Jedgar Kaston was a grade A idiot.

Just in case, though, so as to have a story if he needed one, he stopped in the outer office of this floor – it was the forty seventh – and used the inter-office phone.

"Manager Nellinger?" said the robot in answer to his query. "He has been out-office all morning but is expected back momentarily."

"So that let's me out," said Hook, and broke the connection.

Now all he had to do was go back to Interstell-Imp via Churferen's flier and get Pera. Then he'd take the money-metal Kaston had offered him together with a ticket off-planet. It was all nice and neat and tidy.

So, being Ryder Hook, he decided to have a damned good meal on GCC.

Most operatives would be haring for the exit and wouldn't breathe easily until they had a block between them and GCC. Hook ambled down to the engineer's canteen on the twentieth floor and strolled in, licking his lips in anticipation.

A twenty eight hour service was run here. Hook settled down to study the menu. Hmm! A bewildering range and variety of courses were available. The delicacies of a hundred thousand planets, the best from the cuisines of as many solar systems, were available — and more — to be selected. That the food was synthetically-produced if it was not Lerdunese meant nothing. Synthetic-food — from algae, from grasses, from trees — had kept Old Earth from starving more than once during her periods of population explosion. Once energy could be tapped from fusion power, and later by direct power-taps to the stars themselves, production and energy problems had vanished. Hook selected a Forvash steak, with onions, and dressings, and the knowledge that only moments before it appeared through the slot onto his table it had been part of a great cauldron of basic staples, ready to be manufactured into any one of that hundred thousand more potential dishes, worried him not one whit. It tasted delicious and it contained all the proteins and vitamins he needed.

The red wine he selected to go with it had, moments before, been a base alcohol in the vats. His bottle was prepared and passed up the anti-grav chutes, maturing all the way — all the way!

Even so, Hook still relished, as he had that breakfast, the delights of real meat and real eggs. On a planet that had no chickens — and there were a few in this amazing galaxy — the eggs would be prepared from the cauldrons and appear on the table and no man alive could tell the difference from an egg laid that morning by a real live chicken.

You didn't even need an organic base from which to manufacture proteins for they could be spun polymer-like from sea water and mud and rocks in a few-seconds of processing that encompassed what nature had taken millions of years to perform.

Hook wiped his lips with the napkin and laid it down and felt far more at peace with the galaxy.

Hoffder and Gertrude would be waking up soon, for Hook knew to a nicety how much his blows were worth, and he hoped before they untangled themselves they would realise this was the beginning of a beautiful friendship. He'd better make a move. The meal had been very good. Still and all, he was fully alert with his wits about him.

A tingling all along his organo-metal bones brought Hook quiveringly alive at the table.

He sat there, thrilling and jumping, his nerve-endings streaming billions of messages, his brain speeding into a near-super-human level of activity. How he dreaded this experience! How he longed and hungered for this experience!

A Boosted Man had come within the sphere of mutual inter-relation.

A Boosted Man was nearby!

Hook pushed up from the table. He knew that he could walk quite slowly across to the exit, taking care his coverall did not explode from friction into flames, and the people around him would sit as though lifeless, not seeing him, carrying on their existence at speeds far below those which had become normal to him. His brain raced. Few computers could keep up with him. A Boosted Man! At once he knew the Boosted Man must be Nellinger, the planetary manager for GCC.

This was different.

This was lethal.

The Boosted Men might know of Hook's existence. They might not. He didn't know if they were aware of him in the galaxy. All they would know was that he had been the first volunteer to go on RCI's Powerman Project from which he had been ignominiously turned out. They had followed him on that Project, and gone through to the end and been adapted into men who were no longer ordinary men.

Hook was only half a Boosted Man.

What had been done to their metabolism had changed the Boosted Men's bodies into semi-human forms. Oh, they still looked like human beings, but their skeletons were near-metallic and their muscles and bodily functions had been souped-up to near-superhuman levels. And, gradually, these non-human aspects had taken over their minds. They had become a breed of men apart, the Boosted Men, and they had taken over RCI and Hook knew they intended to take over any and everything in the galaxy they could.

Hook had participated in something of this process, the guinea-pig, the one who had taken the risks to see if the Project was viable. Even he was not aware of all the side-effects. But he had been thrown out. He knew he had lightning-fast reflexes and phenomenal speed in thought-processes. But, he was not a superman. He was an ordinary man; but extraordinary tough and determined, ruthless, possessed, cunning and skilful.

The extra powers conferred on Hook by his Boosting Process were absent at all times except when he came into proximity with another Boosted Man. This was akin to two tuned crystals vibrating when brought together. When he came within the orbit of a Boosted Man – Hook became a Boosted Man himself. It was an experience he feared and loved, that he detested and longed for.

Prometheus cast down out of flames into flames!

Tantalus forever scrabbling for powers that made him a devil or a god!

Hook could be endowed with incredibly speedy thought processes, wide-ranging and all-encompassing, he could multiply enormously the power of his muscles, his bodily functions and speeds could climb prodigiously, his awareness of self and of his surroundings reached hypersensitive proportions – many attributes of the superman could be Hook's – but only when he was in proximity to another Boosted Man whose powers were identical and who was fanatically inimicable to Hook and all his fumbling aspirations!

Truly, he was caught on a cleft stick most painfully thrust between his legs.

To hell with the Boosted Men! They had ruined a dozen planets in the Z'dorangian system. A billion souls had perished on Sterkness and Janitra. They maintained a slave army so sunk in fear they had become mindless zombies. Hook knew much of the evil the Boosted Men had wrought in the galaxy since their creation – and he, Ryder Hook, the very first of them! But – only half a Boosted Man. He with all humility recognised that he did have at least half of common humanity clinging in remnants to him.

He walked quite slowly and carefully out of the engineers' canteen. He could sense the direction of the Boosted Man. He walked that way, through a foyer and past anti-grav chutes, along corridors flooded with the lambent pale-green illumination favoured by the lighting consultants hereabouts, past offices and facilities, past storerooms and warehouses, going higher and higher, following the lodestone he recognised with every atom of his transformed being.

RCI had created the Boosted Men out of ignorance of what they were doing. The Boosted Men had taken over RCI as the day follows the night – or, rather, hating RCI as he did he yet must correct the analogy for the proportions of evil – as the night follows the day.

Now a Boosted Man was here, on Lerdun, lording it over this planetary agency of GCC. That meant only one thing. GCC must be poised to make an attempt upon Interstell-Imp and all the other multi-system conglomerate outlets here – for the greater glory of the Boosted Men and their dark designs, never for poor fumbling back-water RCI – once the proudest of the galaxy's econorgs.

The Boosted Men, Hook knew, liked to call themselves the Novamen.

In a short passageway between an arcade of shops and a swimming pool in the recreation area of the building Hook took the arm of a passing man. It had to be a Homo sapiens, really; Hook had disguised himself as Krifman and even as a mal with plastic tubular ears and a face stretched to breaking point. Terrans of Homo sapiens derivation were easiest.

"What do you want, cretin?" said the man, before Hook knuckled him gently behind the ear and dragged him into the lavatory. Inside the booth Hook began at once. Without his Boosted powers he would have spent perhaps ten seconds considering. Now he had spent all the time he needed considering and could act, and no one could have measured the time interval.

The disguise box in the bottom of his electronics kit yielded facial-gel and hair and cosmetics. Again he did not bother to tint his eyes, leaving them their usual brilliant brown. He turned himself into a passable imitation of the man lying unconscious before him. He stripped off his lime green coverall and transferred the contents of its pockets to the man's lime green metal-fab tunic with the flared skirt. Lime-green trousers were tucked into Hook's own black boots. He checked the man's badge. More ornate than the engineer's, it indicated a higher rank. He could do nothing about the wrist credit-card; but that told him the man was a sales sub-exec responsible for promotion of chemicals and dyes. With his Boosted Powers there was ample time for Hook to strip away the Delling on the man's right wrist and connect up the neural input channels and the electronic outputs. He tested the little gun three times and each time it connected dead square into his hand, the trigger on the last hair's breadth of pressure.

The guy wore metal-fab clothes. That meant he was ready for a gel-mix, for the metal-fab protected the wearer against that ghastly melting effect of the little guns. Only his hands and his face were unprotected. The guy would have hung his hat with the moveable visor on his regular peg. Hook wouldn't bother with that. He took what he required from his electronics kit and stashed the bag on top of a cubicle. The unconscious man was taped up and thrust onto a seat and the door was tumble-locked on him as Hook left.

When he stepped back into that short corridor an observer would have seen Hook enter and then almost immediately leave the lavatory.

Giving a tug to the metal-fab lapel of the low-zipped tunic, Hook swung purposefully along to the executives' grav-shaft elevator.

He had a call to pay on one Nellinger – a Boosted Man.

CHAPTER TWELVE

THE metal-fab clothes did not burn at the speeds Hook chose to use. His processing protected his bare skin. No other reason for him to act as he was acting occurred to him apart from his natural reactions when faced with a poisonous evil that would destroy all with whom it came into contact.

Quite without his own volition his persona as Jack Kinch seeped into the mind that raced away. Jack Kinch had carried out very few assassinations in the galaxy; but his name had become a byword for the impossible. Hook detested the very concept of assassination. He had been convinced by heads which in those days had been wiser than his that sometimes a political assassination worked for the common good. Hook's protest that this merely removed one evil and allowed another to rise in its place was met by the reply that, if a lesser evil could not replace the greater, then the next evil must be removed.

"Until there's no one left?" asked a properly sarcastic Hook.

"That means, then, you believe there are no men of integrity left in the galaxy?"

"Trust me to put my foot in my mouth."

Ryder Hook stood in the elevator, having slowed down as he approached. A Riffian said: "Who the hell are you, taynor?" and had opened his mouth to raise an alarm. With the speed that blurred him into invisibility, Hook whipped around the elevator cage and knuckled all seven occupants. He left at the guard floor at speed.

These people would shudder to their souls if they knew Jack Kinch was aprowl amongst them.

The guard floor protected the levels above where Nellinger had his being.

106

Hook whistled through without being seen.

At the end he smashed the glass over the alarm control board and switched the alarms off. Those goons out there, polishing their guns, reading the transcripts, watching the races on their tvs, would see the glass smash and erupt and the switches go down. By that time Hook would have been back through here, successful – or would never return, being dead of a Boosted Man's powers used utterly ruthlessly against him.

Only one man had the power to stop him now. Nellinger. The Novaman.

But that painful old irony persisted. The one man who could stop him was the one man who was his target. No one else counted.

Hook went through sybaritic luxury, seeing men and aliens in the frozen positions of pleasure and relaxation, passing them as a starship on ftl passes the stars on her route.

Cutting out the alarms had been a little insurance. A Boosted Man – and Hook was now a Boosted Man complete although he would not call himself a Novaman – could be through the alarm area, do what he had come here to do, and whistle back long before the alarms had time to register and arouse the normal-time guards. But Hook had his reasons.

His mind had devised methods of dealing with Nellinger if he found the planetary manager doing any number of a hundred different things. They included finding him doing the merely obvious, like signing his mail, right through to rollicking in bed with a nubile secretary.

Nellinger, of course, was going to be on normal-time when Hook met up with him, and that meant Hook might have to slow to normal-time for a fractional moment so as not to alarm Nellinger. Where Hook could whip around a room filled with normals on slow-time and never be seen, even if the Boosted Man was on slow-time, his processing would enable him to see Hook travelling at boosted-time. This was a matter stored, appreciated and decided upon in micro-seconds in his racing brain.

The penultimate door was an electronic-eye operated sliding door. Had Hook rushed it full-tilt he would have been through the beam and bouncing off the door long before it had time to cycle open. He slowed, broke the beam, the door began to open.

The guard – a Krifman with a broken-nose worn as a badge of honour – shoved upright, gawking.

"Where did you come –?" he began.

Hook kicked him in the guts and speeded up again, shot through the door.

That door, at his present speed, would remain open for a long long time.

You stepped on a poisonous pest, didn't you? You had to deal with a Boosted Man who was destroying all that was good and of life in the galaxy, didn't you? Hook had no doubts what the Boosed Men would do to him if they caught him.

The last door was guarded by three beings. One was Homo sapiens, one was a Krifman, the third was a La'chorite.

Hook slowed.

Three guns appeared – one in a five-fingered human fist, the second in a five-fingered Krifman power-grip, the third in a grip-pouch. Hook watched all three. At the moment when the triggers were pressed almost – almost – to their limits and the contacts would be made, he speeded up and shot right-handed. A tonota Forty scorched through the open door beyond. A Marker Burner followed, visibly lagging behind the Tonota which, although a Forty and thus having only the square-root of the power of an Eighty, still packed tremendous punch. The third gun belched a livid string of power-impulses which, from Hook's boosted speed, looked like a string of lead sausages. The image did not amuse him. One of those lead sausages could en-globe a being and suck every atom of water from his body-tissues instantly, drop him a dessicated husk to the floor, where he'd break into drifting dust.

Hook knuckled each one, the Human and the Krifman be-hind the ear, the La'chorite in the small of the back. They hung in mid-air, already unconscious, but at normal-time taking ages to fall to the floor. He took the Tonota Forty.

Hook slowed, the door opened, and he walked through in slow-time.

The only robots he had seen had been long ago passed.

The robot now confronting him buzzed inquiringly.

Hook shot the Tonota Forty and blew the robot into a spray of nuts and bolts, transistors, printed circuits, and jelly.

The damn thing would have taped his conversation, recorded his voice prints, his photograph, his brain-wave patterns, his heart rhythms, his hair-cell structure, his perspiration, and filed them away for later reference. The abstract of the robot's findings would have gone up on Nellinger's screen, so that the Boosted Man would know who was calling on him.

Hook stepped past.

No normal man could have reached where Hook had reached bent on the purpose on which he was bent.

The RCI Powerman Project had been exactly that, to power a man, not to power a man's tools and weapons and artefacts. Hook believed that any man in Nellinger's position would have a really hefty power-gun in his office, a weapon that could knock holes in the walls and smash the place to pieces and set it into an inferno. A trick like that wouldn't worry a Boosted Man when his neck was at stake – as, probably, it wouldn't worry the most ordinary of men faced with his own dissolution.

Outside this luxury suite, now, for instance, the twin blasts from the Forty and the Burner had merely sprayed in flame off the armoured walls through the door. But Nellinger wouldn't quibble at using, say, a Tonota Eighty or a Martian Mega up here. It behooved Hook to hit first; for even a Boosted Man, running at top speed, could not outrun the speed of light.

On a windowsill Hook noticed a delightful Ph'iang ceramic bowl filled with forget-me-nots. Real honest-to-goodness terrestrial forget-me-nots. They bloomed there in shy sweet beauty and they brought a remembered pang to Ryder Hook. But the forget-me-nots had no power now to soften Hook's heart.

He only wished they had.

A girl's light laugh rang out ahead, gay, light-hearted, unaffected. Hook shook his head.

"Dear old Dirty Berti Bashti!" he said. "He has got a girl with him."

Being Ryder Hook he did not close his eyes. But that would have been a normal reaction in that moment in that superbly luxurious apartment. Luxury – well, that was what it was all about. For money and power men would do anything, so Hook had discovered, and when you boiled it all down and deducted the sheer perverted pleasure some men got from holding power over others and moving events, what men did it for was luxury.

The periods he had spent in slow time after first passing through the alarm system had added up now to a sizeable amount. Hook knew to the exact micro-second how long he had left.

There would be no long-drawn-out confrontation between these two Boosted Men. No one would be allowed into these private apartments unless sent for by Nellinger. There would be no long scene of clever backchat with each explaining his position, with perhaps some bargaining, a deal, a surprise, a struggle. The moment Nellinger caught sight of Hook he would shoot.

Instantly.

A Boosted Man's hearing was phenomenal. Hook could hear the girl laughing clear through all the intervening rooms of the apartment. He could also hear the two people moving about. They were moving normally. Hook – well, he moved like a savage barbarian, perfectly soundlessly. That had not come with the Powerman Project. That was Ryder Hook. He could reach to within about six metres of the Boosted Man before Nellinger picked up his breathing, the sound of his clothes, the inescapable slight scuff of his boots. Hook could, of course, simply burn down everything before him. Set the Tonota Forty on full power and burn and burn and burn. He could get away easily enough from the apartment before it all burned. But he wouldn't be sure that would succeed.

Ryder Hook was not a man to commit suicide lightly.

Once Nellinger was dead all his Boosted Men's powers would die with him. There would be no resonating crystal to vibrate its opposite number. Hook would no longer be a Boosted Man. Once more a physically normal human being on slow-time what chance would he stand of escaping this nest alive?

None.

He moved forward carefully.

He was fully conscious of his reluctance to kill Nellinger and thus deprive himself, Ryder Hook, of these drug-like powers. How well he could understand just why the Boosted Men had grown insane with ambition! He could not guarantee that if he possessed the Novaman's powers all the time he, too, would not

110

have joined them. A Boosted Man tasted the most subtle and most powerful drug ever invented.

He heard the girl walking towards him. Her footsteps by the lightness and springiness of their tread told Hook what kind of girl she would be, her build, her weight. She would be beautiful. A man with Nellinger's power did not surround himself with ugly objects.

Hook stood beside a curtain. The prey was coming to him, then.

The girl entered the room. She was still laughing. She was beautiful. She carried a drink in one hand and the other lightly brushed the tops of tables and chairs, trailed along an ivory of Joinver's Artemis, flicked the pages of a book – it was a hand-printed Uoi'jo'luor, the sacred book of the Joilupri, a sect who owned just two solar systems and were content with them – tinkled the golden bells of a Halpey shrine. The cost of the furnishing and the objets d'art in this room would have bankrupted many a medium-sized business. The girl laughed and trailed a gauzy scarf from her throat, and her white body glowed in hidden roseate lamps and Hook lifted the gun and felt the ugliness of the metal shiver through his own part-metal bones.

"Liri! You she-cat!" Nellinger's voice, thick with passion and drink. They'd been lunching well, then, somewhere romantic across the wide surface of Lerdun.

"I'm here, Ray."

Ray. His name was Ray.

He walked into the room after the girl, only half-laughing, growing just a little tired of this independent romp on Liri's part. He wore a lounging robe of brocaded silk from the C'tang system out beyond Vega way, and he, too, carried a drink. His face showed all the marks of total power and absolute authority. That he was a Boosted Man only the thrilling response from Hook could testify. He reached for the girl and Hook rose up behind him and hit him with the gun-butt.

Nellinger collapsed to the priceless carpet.

The girl did not scream.

She regarded Hook gravely, her violet eyes wide, her mouth half-open and glistening with drink.

"You're a dead man," she said. "You know that."

111

Hook reached out and brushed away one rounded white arm, knuckled her behind the ear. She fell across Nellinger.

Hook felt glad that he had not been forced to kill her. Then he felt the scathing contempt of his own weakness. What was the life of one silly, beautiful girl worth in the balance beside ridding the galaxy of a Boosted Man?

Nothing.

She had certainly thought Nellinger had been killed. Hook had brought the gun-butt down with crushing force. But Hook knew what a Boosted Man's skull was like. That part-metal dome would take sledgehammer force to break. Even now Nellinger was stirring, breathing harshly and raggedly; but already he was coming around from a blow that would have smashed an ordinary man's skull into bloody pulp and bone fragments.

Hook kicked that priceless carpet aside, rucking up a corner away from the inlaid teak and ebony floor. Beneath the floor the armour kept this place inviolate. Hook rolled Nellinger over so that his right hand and arm flung out, resting on the wooden floor, clear of the carpet. The sleeve-mounted gun showed up. It was not a Delling and Hook, to his intense surprise, did not recognise the make. That kind of thing worried him; but he did not hesitate.

The moment Nellinger came around fully he'd activate his neural and electronic circuits and aim to blast Hook down with that little weapon up his sleeve.

Hook aimed the Tonota Forty on low power and crisped off the Novaman's hand above the wrist. The wound cauterised at once. The floor burst into flame and emitted choking black smoke; but the blast bounced at an angle from the armour beneath. Hook put the blaze out by stamping his precious boots on the licking flames.

That priceless carpet had not been harmed.

If Nellinger died, Hook was trapped. There was no gainsaying that.

So far Hook had not had to cut in his EAS organic circuits and patch into whatever apparat network GCC operated out here in this end of the galaxy. The job was tricky – but he could do it. There was no need. He quite enjoyed fooling whoever it was at whatever control he picked up. One day they'd catch on.

112

Then he'd have betrayed just one more facet of his resources and personality.

He fast-timed around the apartment, going from room to room, lost in admiration for the beauty – although a trifle curl-of-the-lip about Nellinger's florid tastes. He found the anti-grav equipment in an elaborately-decorated chest after the fashion of Hactkchk – an unpronounceable name for an alien craftsman of superlative skill – and lifted out a single set. When he got back Liri still slumbered and Nellinger was breathing heavily again. For a third time Hook hit him. Then he strapped on the anti-grav pack, like a waistcoat it fitted around waist and over shoulders and he sticky-zipped it up. It was a big and powerful set, unlike those sets Hook was used to that came in the form of a pack no larger than a man's hand fitted into the small of the back. You could fly around the world on this little beauty.

He hoisted Nellinger up. He remained on speed-time.

He walked towards the window. They were eighty storeys up and it was a long drop. The Tonota Forty bounced off the armour window and Hook cursed. There was nothing else for it but to look again and more carefully for the big energy-gun he was sure the Novaman must have somewhere.

Still on fast-time he looked – and his boosted senses picked up the millimetre misalignment of the glass over a cocktail bar. He swept the glitter of bottles and glasses to the floor. Well – here goes – he shot the glass out.

The frame buckled, shredded, fell. Beyond it – Hook whistled in fresh admiration – beyond the concealing glass lay a chamber massively stocked with weapons. He'd like to spend some time there; but Nellinger moaned again and so had to be put to sleep once more. Hook selected a Martian Mega. He preferred the Mega to the Tonota. With this in his fist and Nellinger over his shoulder he stalked towards the window once again – and paused.

Flashing concepts burned in his mind – not the idea, that was obvious – but the ramifications from his action, as though he played chess and looked from "King's pawn to King four" to the quiet words: "Checkmate" in a single flash of reasoning.

He kept Nellinger on his shoulder and stuck the Martian

Mega under that lime-green tunic. The micro-seconds were ticking away; but there was still time.

The planetary manager had a massively-furnished terminal console and Hook quickly punched up for an interstellar line. He rubbed his jaw reflectively; he would have to come down to slow-time so as to give the computer a chance.

What the computer might think of patching him into a Lerdun government circuit and then of calling up Albeira, Hook didn't care — for he was open-enough-minded to consider that, just maybe, computers did worry over their own business. He dialled out for a person-to-person call to Taynor Porten, tenth-vice-president in charge of systems control. When the communications equipment indicated the call completed — and that took a whaling great chunk out of Hook's time calculations — he punched out "speech."

Porten came up on the screen. He was light years away; but you'd never know. His first words were:

"So you've a deal for me, have you, Nellinger! If this is your idea of secrecy — it isn't mine —"

Then he saw Hook.

"Pera Sotherton," said Hook. He spoke quickly; but he was still in slow-time. "We didn't get off-planet. The government goons fouled us up. I'm Ryder Hook. I've a deal for you. But be quick — you know where I am and this connection is about as security-minded as a colander in a cement-mixer."

"Speak."

"You come to Lerdun and fetch Pera. It is worth your while. You're systems control, you'll know what the deal is."

"You —" Porten regarded him — at least, Hook surmised this from the more agitated movement of the mass of hairs sprouting from the faceted wickerwork basket — "You are Homo sapiens, like Pera. I get on with Earthpeople. But — what deal can you offer —"

Hook sighed. "You know where I am. Isn't that good enough guarantee?"

"Two days — my days — to clear up here and I'm on my way." Porten must have used one of the hair-concealed arms to dial up a secretarial replacement, for he went on: "Patten Starship *Venezia*."

Hook nodded. Like RCI, Pattens were an Earth outfit origin-ally. "I'll be waiting." Then, to give point to what they had been half-saying, and hinting at, he added: "If I'm still alive." He broke the connection and stood back, sprayed the computer with the Tonota Forty. The automatic sprinklers came on and put the fire out – but the computer terminal and its records were finished.

At last he could get on with it.

Hook took a last look around. The rolled back carpet; the un-conscious form of Liri – the wreckage of the arms room past the mirror and the destroyed terminal were out of sight further back in the apartment – the lushness and the luxury of it, and he sighed.

The Martian Mega took the window out with four good hard squirts. Good builders, then. No chance of hiding that from the GCC enforcers. They'd come arunning with weapons in their fists.

Hook stood on the window still, feeling the heat of the melted armour glass pooling about him. The day was still bright and the sun shone bravely. A long way down, eighty storeys.

Looking like a discarded page from an old-fashioned book there lay below him an open area, grassed, with trees and an orn-amental pool, sun glinting. It lay beyond the armoured peri-meter of the GCC complex. Hook balanced on the window sill and launched himself into space. He dropped without activating the anti-grav waistcoat. Nellinger moaned and Hook clamped the fingers of his left hand about the Novaman's neck – and squeezed.

The ground rushed up.

But Hook although he had jumped in boosted-time was now in normal time. The anti-grav could only operate within its de-signed capacity. Normal time ticked by now as Hook fell. Nor-mal time was slow time to a Boosted Man. Normal time gave the guards ample time to rush past the shattered doors and into the apartment and to see Liri sprawled on the floor, the vapour-ised window. Plenty of time to run to the window and look out and down and see Hook dropping away below. Plenty of time.

Whatever thoughts of disbelief clamoured in their heads they were not slow to react in the way typical of econorg enforcers. Weapons sprouted through the shattered window.

If they believed they had only to aim their guns and press the triggers or thumb the studs and so dispose of the man dropping away below them, they were sadly astray in their reckoning. That they would shoot, Hook knew; they would scarcely understand that the inert lump he carried flung over a shoulder was their boss, the potent planetary manager Nellinger.

Hook lifted the Martian Mega and fired.

Most of the window that had been left and much of the masonry whiffed away into a boiling spout of super-heated gases and free electrons. The guards disappeared in that supernal flare of energy. Hook dropped lower, in free fall, plummeting to the ground.

No one else put their head through the window to take a shot at him.

He estimated the rate the ground was coming up, the distance to go, and at precisely the right time he activated the anti-grav waistcoat.

His fall checked, he hung fleetingly in balance, staring up just in case some goon took a reckless chance and looked out. His boosted sight perfectly and clearly picked out every detail of the window he had ruined and of the adjoining windows. No one.

He started a gentle descent and felt a sudden and savage blow rip up his back. Only his movement in resuming the drop had saved him. Someone from below had shot at him. He glanced down and was aware instantly of the speed the ground was flashing up towards him.

He grabbed for the anti-grav control dials and twisted up full power. He continued to drop. That blow ripping up his back had smashed the anti-grav mechanism.

He was plunging helplessly down to the ground, from a distance of at least thirty metres, hurtling down towards instant destruction.

All his Boosted senses now could only add to the agony of the moment.

When he hit that ground it would be the finish for Ryder Hook – one time adventurer of the galaxy – presumptive corpse.

CHAPTER THIRTEEN

THE ground roared up at him and the wind smashed and blustered past, billowing his trousers and streaming his hair. There was little time left.

Ryder Hook was still a Boosted Man.

He let that relentlessly choking grip around Nellinger's throat relax. He hit the man across the chin, hard, twice. He gripped the Novaman by the front of his robe and lowered the unconscious body. Bending double, Hook wrapped both feet around the man's neck, pressing in, resting the soles of those black boots of his on Nellinger's shoulders. He squeezed his feet together.

Like a doubled-up arrow the two men pitched down through empty air.

Hook eased his sideways pressure just a trifle, just enough to let air into Nellinger's lungs but not enough to let the Novaman slip away from between those talon-like feet.

In the screaming bluster of wind Nellinger moaned and, after all the punishment he had taken, after those last two wicked blows from Hook, he regained consciousness. Crouching atop him, Hook grasped his left hand into the Boosted Man's hair and rode him down as a Kamikaze rode his rocket nuclear-warhead down.

"Nellinger!" Hook yelled. "Boosted Man! You're going to hit!"

Nellinger looked down.

Hook had judged it perfectly.

The Boosted Man reacted. He writhed, his legs thrusting out – and in that split-micro-second as they struck, so Ryder Hook stood upright on the Boosted Man's shoulders – and jumped.

He kicked hard with both cruel feet, jumped straight upwards.

Nellinger's feet hit the ground. His legs telescoped and broke free of the hip joints, speared up into his body. His backbone compacted and bent and snapped. His head sank down between his shoulder blades. He squashed.

Hook's last split-micro-second leap carried his body fractionally upwards – all his strength was spent in countering the inertial forces impelling him to smash into the ground and follow Nellinger's disintegration. He hurtled forward, tucked his head in, and rolled. He went over and over like an insane tumbleweed eight times before he cannoned into the low wall surrounding the park.

He was winded, his body felt as though he'd been whiplashed over a limber-wheel, everything inside him felt loose.

Even then, in that instant of insane release, he was aware of the dying tingling in his body, of the exact instant that Ray Nellinger, planetary manager, Boosted Man, had ceased to live. Hook was able to investigate the interesting fact that his own powers did not die on that instant of the other's dissolution as he had expected; but he felt his Boosted powers slowly seeping from him and thereby was both marvellously exhilarated and terrifyingly dismayed.

To be a Boosted Man!

Unholy joy and unholy terror!

He was in normal time now as he sat up and, quite automatically, dived sideways.

The blast bit a chunk the size of a gravestone out of the low wall. The Martian Mega belched once and the man shooting at him, the stone wall from which he had been firing, the tree beside him, everything blazed and vapourised and melted.

Hook ran and jinked and ran and jinked the other way. No one else shot at him as he cleared the park. He dropped his run down to a smart walk as he came out onto the boulevard and in his own time strolled off. He was aware of one or two quizzical looks at the mess on his back. At the first public disposall he stripped off the anti-grav waistcoat. The thing had been torn as though savaged in the jaws of a tiger, and the delicate circuits exposed themselves like a black and twisted forest after a fire. He dropped the waistcoat down the disposall.

Back at GCC they'd be setting up a search pattern. At first

they'd be wondering what had happened to manager Nellinger, and that might slow them down a trifle. As soon as the gruesome remains in the park had been given a positive ID the next in line at GCC would take over.

Time, Ryder Hook said to himself confidently, for him to reach Interstell-Imp and manager Kaston.

He fished out the speaker and the mike and re-inserted them in ear and mouth respectively.

At once: "Goddammed terrestrial plug-ugly curd of a bastard! Hook!"

He took out the spy eye and fastened it on the lime-green tunic.

"So you're on the street! What's been happening?"

"Once I get to Churferen and the flier is well away, I'll give you a full report."

"It had better be good! If you've been double –"

"Now, Kaston, do you think I'd do that with Tayniss Sotherton in her present predicament?"

"Just remember."

In the next quarter of an hour Hook further ran his time limits into the red by again detaching the spy eye, the speaker and the mike and walking confidently into a satellite post office. The place was a Lerdun government department, of course; but Hook used money-metal which he had found to his pleased acceptance in the tunic pocket. He deposited the pearl hologram, all wrapped and sealed in a safe-box that would open only to his thumbprint on the plasticpanel. Then he walked out, whistling, donned Kaston's apparat equipment once again and headed out for Churferen.

During the flier ride his aches and pains vanished and he was back to full one hundred and one percent by the time he once again faced planetary manager Jedgar Kaston. This time it was a flesh and blood mal he spoke to – flesh and blood and all the scientific wizardry of pseudo-life that made up a dynaman.

"You sent me what I wanted to know, Hook. We shall move against GCC – soon." Kaston's face betrayed no emotion. Hook had been searched, of course, before he entered here. The little Delling had not been unstrapped and uncircuited from his wrist; they'd merely inserted a back-plug which ensured that if he fired the thing it would explode and gel-mix would dissolve his own arm. The Martian Mega and the Zag had been taken from him.

Hook had to say what was expected of him.

"I've kept my part of the bargain – and you got Nellinger as well. That's a bonus."

"Nothing is a bonus when I pay for it. You delivered what you were employed to do." The dynaman's torso leaned forward in the cocoon. "I'm interested in how you did it."

"As we planned. I had to take your electronics gear out. I felt sure it was being monitored."

"If it was," Kaston said, and his mallian face abruptly betrayed a curl of contempt, "it didn't slow you down."

"No," said Ryder Hook, quondam half a Boosted Man. "No, I can't say it slowed me down."

Pera Sotherton was escorted in by the woman in the white apron. The woman's gun was holstered; but the quick-release flap was open and her hand never strayed far from the butt.

"Oh! Hook! You're still alive!"

"A habit I believe in. You're all I.Q.?"

"Yes. I've been waiting and wondering –"

"Save it," said Hook. It shouldn't be this easy.

"You, Ryder Hook," said Kaston, "are a very dangerous man. I really cannot have you running about the galaxy at will." He flicked a tentacle and four enforcers appeared at the door. "If you would be good enough to go through what happened in detail . . ."

"Like I said," said Hook, speaking easily, poised. "You planned it. I did it. What more is there."

Kaston sighed. "A very great deal more, I know. But I have much to do – the push against GCC demands total effort and concentration. And I do not trust you. You will have to go."

"Thank the Great Salvor –" said Pera.

Hook said nothing. They were led out. If Pera woke up to what was really planned for them before he had time to alter the plan she would be a hindrance. How in this goddam galaxy had he got mixed up with her in the first place? Come to that, what the blue blazing hell had he come back to Interstell-Imp for? To get Pera out? He was going soft. There could be no doubt of that.

Hook had to give Jedgar Kaston credit. The dynaman had ordered an easy and quick death for them and had refrained from sending them to one of his more refined deaths by torture. Maybe the mal had a glimmer of humanity, after all.

They were taken down to a plain white-panelled cell where the woman left. She didn't speak much. The four enforcers un-limbered their guns. They were a blank-faced bunch, aliens from out Spica way, tough and unscrupulous and ruthless. Their trouble was that Ryder Hook was a great deal more tough and unscrupulous and ruthless than they were.

He let Pera walk towards the door in the back wall – that door through which so many people had thought they would be walking to freedom and where the goons would chop them down. He lingered.

"Don't you wanna go, gonil?"

"Of course I want to go!" said Hook, and added a vastly objectionable and crude comment. "But I need to go to the lavatory first."

His left hand had not ceased to work on the back-plugged Delling. The technical problem was simple; difficulty was the ejection of the plug without it falling and betraying him. He curled his fingers around it, easing, and by a millimetre it came free.

"You won't need toilet facilities where you're going, curd," said another of the Spicans.

"I usually like to wipe clean," said Hook, and lifted his right hand and moved and fired, three times, and then stood stock-still as the three revolting piles of collapsing jelly sloughed and shrivelled on the neat white plastic floor.

"*Hook!*"

"Act your age, Pera! Look at them."

He had hit the faces of the three aliens. Their metal-fab clothing had not protected them. It lay now, empty and oozing, and the three weapons lay on the plastic. He wasn't going to pick up one of those guns. They were covered with gel-mix.

"They were going to shoot us, Hook! Oh –" She swayed.

121

Hook didn't bother to put an arm around her waist. He was too busy working on the door. When it opened they went through, with Pera hanging onto his left arm. The passageway led through a guardroom where, shortly thereafter, only deliquescing masses of jelly dripped from chairs and bunks. Hook selected a Tonota Eighty – the guardroom did not boast a Martian Mega – and blew a hole in the doorway leading out. Four quick blasts cleared the next area. When they ran through the smoke and flame and pelted down a flight of steps there lay before them, blue in the dusk, one of the neat and evening-thronged boulevards of Cantacle.

They walked along together, side by side. Hook was busy checking the back trail and so could not spare the effort of putting his arm around Pera's waist. They walked on.

"We've got to hide somewhere Pera. Find fresh clothes and disguises. We've got to get to Pearlhampton to meet Porten."

"Taynor Porten will keep his word."

"I just hope so. He's the only chance we've got, and he's the joker in the pack."

"He may not be a Homo sapiens, Hook; but he's a gentleman."

"Good for him," said Ryder Hook. "I'm not and I don't pretend to be."

"It's no secret," said Pera Sotherton, and her nose went into the air.

Hook was used to fending for himself in the galaxy, having a girl along did not help. Later that evening he walked past a patrolling Lerdun government goon – they had the temerity to call them planetary police – and, swinging swiftly about, chopped him down. The goon lay unconscious. Hook took his pocketbook and loose change. He did this three times, and then they had enough for a room down where the dregs of society hung out. Even in this modern galaxy of the hundred and first century there were the down-and-outers, of whom Hook knew much, people of all races and shapes and sizes who had not made a go of it. Once you were turned out of your econorg you would be extraordinarily fortunate to be taken by any other; you could be a spy, couldn't you?

At last Hook could say to Pera: "Patten starship *Venezia* is due in at Pearlhampton tomorrow, Pera."

They had new clothes, new faces, new identities. They had money metal that had warmed the pockets of government goons.

"The Lerdun government put me in this mess," said Hook, "By their intransigence. I'm merely balancing the books – and not by much, either." He remembered Giffler.

Porten of Pattens had arranged with HGL's agency on Lerdun for safe-conduct for their starship *Venezia*. Trade and business deals were the life-blood of the galaxy. All the econorgs knew that Porten must be up to something; but they felt secure, for no multi-system conglomerate had much of a chance of opening up operations on a planet so well served by econorgs already there. So Porten could arrange a mutual with HGL and space in. Maybe he was taking a holiday.

Hook and Pera waited inconspicuously in arrivals at Pearlhampton's second spaceport. The first carried most-favoured ships, and although HGL was a most-favoured econorg, this mutual with Pattens carried no such credit. The sun shone down through the transparent roof; many people were there to greet arrivals from a hundred worlds in space, spaceships were taking off and leaving in a gratifyingly trouble-free pattern. Hook bought Pera an ice-cream and she sucked it thoroughly. A nice little spot of local camouflage colour, that was what that ice-cream was to Ryder Hook.

"Patten starship *Venezia* has just made touchdown," came the modulated tones over the speakers. "Passengers will be arriving at gate Baker-Blue momentarily." No one took much notice. These people had nothing to do with Pattens.

Hook and Pera moved forward. From the blue-painted gate came the passengers from the transporter. Because of the absence of any other welcome a space had formed. Hook frowned. He could see the wicker-work form of Porten gliding on those all-but invisible legs, he could see half a dozen other Kirchers with their Kircher boss. Other aliens walked or glided or hopped in Porten's party; but the majority were Krifmans and Homo sapiens. A mal dynaman floated on his anti-gravs with the party, and Hook gave Porten a point. A useful ally to have along when

123

he would be dealing with a mal dynaman.

Pera ran forward, holding out her arms, and Hook wondered just what kind of special relationship would develop – had developed – between the beautiful terrestrial girl and the perambulating wickerwork basket covered in hair. Whatever it was, it was all a part of the ftl life glittering away in the whirlpool of stars.

A man in a black uniform walked across to Hook. He had his right hand resting on the butt of his gun. His face showed a replica of the look of absolute triumphant pleasure Hook had seen there before. In the man's left hand a small sensing device indicated just how he had become so victoriously sure of his quarry.

Hook's face with its heavy disguise remained blank. The black uniformed man halted before Hook. He was enjoying this.

"Ryder Hook, I believe?"

"Sure," said Hook, and drew his gun and shot Goton Telander's guts out through his backbone.

Panic and uproar, chaos of screaming and running, complete disorganisation burned through the reception area. Hook sprinted across to Porten and on the way dropped three of Telander's enforcers who tried to shoot him. He grabbed Pera around the waist.

"Taynor Porten! Get your people away from here, fast!"

"But you're not the man who –" began Porten.

"This is Ryder Hook," said Pera. "Who else would it be creating all this trouble?"

They ran out to the waiting cars arranged by HGL and screamed off towards Pearlhampton.

Hook worked feverishly changing his disguise, turning himself into an old man with a frizz of hair. His skull-shape changed under layers of facial-gel. "Get me the clothes of that guy in the back, Pera."

The taynor pointed out, fat, elderly, clutching a metalloy briefcase, yelped: "I'm sixteenth vice-president. You're not having my clothes."

"Do as Ryder Hook says," said Porten in a voice that made everyone except Hook jump.

At the satellite post office Hook was dropped off and in the sixteenth vice-president's clothes, his back bowed and with a car-cushion stuffed up the front of his tunic, he shuffled up the steps. His thumb-print remained his own and the safety-box duly flicked out of the chute into his waiting palm.

Outside, on the sun-baked boulevard, the Lerdun goons were being offensive to the Patten party parked in their cars. Hook waited and watched. Patten was not the same easy meat as a loner in the galaxy. HGL would go to bat for Porten, for a big deal hung on this. The police, unable to prove that Porten's party had any connection with the spaceport incident – "We drove off because we had no wish to become involved," – had to let them go. Hook heard Porten say in parting: "Rest assured, officer, your superiors will be apprised of this."

He chuckled. He rather liked old Porten – and that was a strange business for him. He wandered along to the hotel and some of Porten's people smuggled him in. Then it was a mere matter of waiting. With the pearl hologram yielding up the secrets of Interstell-Imp and particularly of Jedgar Kaston, Hook knew that the Lerdun government would be forced to move. HGL would be in on the deal, and GCC, too, until they were ready for the chop.

In the event, as Hook learned lying on a comfortable bed in the hotel and drinking champagne, Interstell-Imp were taken in the act of raping GCC. Kaston's coup had succeeded admirably. Then Porten had taken Kaston's Interstell-Imp agency and with it, GCC, also.

They all said how great a day it was. They added that it had all been easy because planetary manager Ray Nellinger had so unfortunately fallen to his death. The sixteenth vice-president had the grace to add, once more in his own clothes, that he supposed if it hadn't been for Ryder Hook they couldn't have done it.

Hook waved his champagne glass.

"Think nothing of it."

Then what he had said sobered him. They would think nothing of it. Pera said, eagerly: "I'm sure Mr. Porten will ask you to join Patten, Hook. You'll have a real credit card!"

Being Ryder Hook, he didn't say: "Big deal." But those were his sentiments.

"I don't think so, Pera. I'd be tied down. I'd be restricted –"

"But you'd be secure!"

"Maybe. But security and me don't mix too well."

She sat up on the bed. Her dark hair was tousled. She was remarkably beautiful. "I think you're a – a great chancroid and a burst ulcer and I don't know what!"

"And you're a girl who would want all the things I couldn't give you." He tweaked her ear. "I'm not sure I'd give 'em to you if I could."

"So you're going off again, spacing out, taking off for the galaxy."

"I believe so. Anyway, I have a feeling it's time I looked up Shaeel. Ve's a great guy – or gal." He chuckled. "Shaeel can aspirate as good an 'H' as you or I. Yet ve always says 'ook. It's always 'ook."

"I'll give you 'ook," said Ts Pera Sotherton and jumped on him. Hook chuckled and rolled away and grabbed her and thereafter, had he been in the mind, might have found a very good reason to stay on with Patten.

He did not.

Ryder Hook was a loner in this magic, brilliant, brutal whirlpool of stars.

Porten set him up with new clothes, a bulging pocket book with money metal that would take him plenty of parsecs, and a ticket aboard HGL starship *Maquinchao*. Pera came down to the spaceport to see him off, and this time, with Pattens and HGL hovering invisibly over them in protection, there was no harassment from the Lerdun government. Anyway, Hook looked like a senior vice-president, with greying hair and a met-alloy rat-trap for a mouth. He had the loading robots carry his dunnage aboard, all new, all expensive, and all loaded down with goodies Pera had pressed on him.

"Hook –" She suddenly saw the sly look in his brown eyes and her chin went up. "Pattens have taken over the agencies here. We've done all right. But you turn your back on all this and go off to the galaxy, you great chancroid!"

"You're rather sweet yourself," said Hook, and kissed her and so left her there.

Even then, he wasn't so sure that one evil had not replaced another – but – nothing could be more evil than a Boosted Man, could it? Ryder Hook had to hold onto that belief as he took off into the whirlpool of stars.

NEL BESTSELLERS

Crime

T012 484	FIVE RED HERRINGS	*Dorothy L. Sayers*	40p
T015 556	MURDER MUST ADVERTISE	*Dorothy L. Sayers*	40p
T014 398	STRIDING FOLLY	*Dorothy L. Sayers*	30p

Fiction

T015 386	THE NORTHERN LIGHT	*A. J. Cronin*	50p
T016 544	THE CITADEL	*A. J. Cronin*	75p
T015 130	THE MONEY MAKER	*John J. McNamara Jr.*	50p
T013 820	THE DREAM MERCHANTS	*Harold Robbins*	75p
T018 105	THE CARPETBAGGERS	*Harold Robbins*	95p
T016 560	WHERE LOVE HAS GONE	*Harold Robbins*	75p
T013 707	THE ADVENTURERS	*Harold Robbins*	80p
T006 743	THE INHERITORS	*Harold Robbins*	60p
T009 467	STILETTO	*Harold Robbins*	30p
T015 289	NEVER LEAVE ME	*Harold Robbins*	40p
T016 579	NEVER LOVE A STRANGER	*Harold Robbins*	75p
T011 798	A STONE FOR DANNY FISHER	*Harold Robbins*	60p
T015 874	79 PARK AVENUE	*Harold Robbins*	75p
T011 461	THE BETSY	*Harold Robbins*	80p
T013 340	SUMMER OF THE RED WOLF	*Morris West*	50p

Historical

T013 758	THE LADY FOR RANSOM	*Alfred Duggan*	40p
T015 297	COUNT BOHEMOND	*Alfred Duggan*	50p
T010 279	MASK OF APOLLO	*Mary Renault*	50p
T014 045	TREASURE OF PLEASANT VALLEY	*Frank Yerby*	35p
T015 602	GILLIAN	*Frank Yerby*	50p

Science Fiction

T015 017	EQUATOR	*Brian Aldiss*	30p
T014 347	SPACE RANGER	*Isaac Asimov*	30p
T015 491	PIRATES OF THE ASTEROIDS	*Isaac Asimov*	30p
T016 331	THE CHESSMEN OF MARS	*Edgar Rice Burroughs*	40p
T013 537	WIZARD OF VENUS	*Edgar Rice Burroughs*	30p
T009 696	GLORY ROAD	*Robert Heinlein*	40p
T016 900	STRANGER IN A STRANGE LAND	*Robert Heinlein*	75p
T011 844	DUNE	*Frank Herbert*	75p
T012 298	DUNE MESSIAH	*Frank Herbert*	40p
T015 211	THE GREEN BRAIN	*Frank Herbert*	30p

War

T013 367	DEVIL'S GUARD	*Robert Elford*	50p
T015 505	THE LAST VOYAGE OF GRAF SPEE	*Michael Powell*	30p
T015 661	JACKALS OF THE REICH	*Ronald Seth*	30p
T012 263	FLEET WITHOUT A FRIEND	*John Vader*	30p

Western

T016 994	No. 1 EDGE – THE LONER	*George G. Gilman*	30p
T016 536	No. 5 EDGE – BLOOD ON SILVER	*George G. Gilman*	30p
T017 621	No. 6 EDGE – THE BLUE. THE GREY AND THE RED	*George G. Gilman*	30p
T014 479	No. 7 EDGE – CALIFORNIA KILLING	*George G. Gilman*	30p
T015 254	No. 8 EDGE – SEVEN OUT OF HELL	*George G. Gilman*	30p
T015 475	No. 9 EDGE – BLOODY SUMMER	*George G. Gilman*	30p

General

T011 763	SEX MANNERS FOR MEN	*Robert Chartham*	30p
W002 531	SEX MANNERS FOR ADVANCED LOVERS	*Robert Chartham*	25p
W002 835	SEX AND THE OVER FORTIES	*Robert Chartham*	30p
T010 732	THE SENSUOUS COUPLE	*Dr. 'C'*	25p

NEL P.O. BOX 11, FALMOUTH, TR 10 9EN, CORNWALL

Please send cheque or postal order. Allow 10p to cover postage and packing on one book plus 4p for each additional book.

Name ....

Address ....

....

Title ....